CONFESSIONS

OF A

Call Centre
Worker

CONFESSIONS

OF A

Call Centre
Worker

KRIS YONZONE

RUPA

Published by
Rupa Publications India Pvt. Ltd 2013
7/16, Ansari Road, Daryaganj
New Delhi 110002

Sales centres:
Allahabad Bengaluru Chennai
Hyderabad Jaipur Kathmandu
Kolkata Mumbai

ISBN: 978-81-291-2411-1

10 9 8 7 6 5 4 3 2 1

Typeset in Adobe Garamond 12/16 by Jojy Philip, New Delhi.

Printed at Thomson Press India Ltd, Faridabad.

To Goku and Genghis

CONTENTS

1

WHAT DO YOU WANT TO BE?

'What do you want to be in life?'

That's a question most of you've heard at some time or the other. The first time was probably from the mouth of a teacher. And you probably said you wanted to be a doctor, an engineer, a nurse, a fire-fighter, and so on. Maybe if you liked to be the class kiss-ass or the teacher's pet, you said, 'I want to be a teacher, like you', and got a gold star or a pat on the head. If you did, then shame on you. Go kneel in the corner, and assume the murgasana while you are at it. Unlike some chaps in class who had a predetermined course in life—like my cousin Gautam who knew he was going to be a fighter pilot and watched *Top Gun* almost every day; he also insisted on being called 'Maverick', as if that would expedite his dreams—I never knew what I really wanted to be or do. My answers involved the things I was interested in at that very moment. And since I had the attention span of a goldfish on crack cocaine the answers were always very, um, exotic.

'Miss, I want to be a professional wrestler when I grow up.' That was 1993, and we'd just got cable television. A Canadian wrestler in pink tights would hand out his pink glasses before every match to a kid in the crowd. In hindsight, the wrestler was just a little bit gay; but to my prepubescent mind, he was the epitome of machismo. I wanted to be Kris, Excellence of Execution.

Around class five, it was: 'Sir, I want to be a superhero after a radioactive incident of the gamma ray variety.' I had just watched *Superman*, *Batman* and *The Hulk* in a marathon Hollywood movies session. What kid does not want to be a super-powered freak capable of reducing entire cities to ash with a blink of his eye or a little wind out of the rear end? Note here the bizarre underwear worn by superheroes, which in hindsight is also a little gay. Utterly horrifying to the slightly homophobic adult me, but a source of hours of endless enthralment to pubescent me. I wanted to be Super Kris, Defender of Truth, Justice and Vanilla Ice-cream.

Around class ten, it was: 'Miss, I want to become a lion tamer.' We'd got Discovery Channel and making money while working with wild animals seemed simply awesome. Besides, the chicks found it very sexy

There were many things I wanted to do in life, but none of them were what I wanted to be on a permanent basis. Wrestler, lawyer, actor, singer, lion tamer, male model, stripper, bartender, DJ, bouncer, ninja robot operator, professional party animal—they were all on my list. Then reality set in and I woke up to the fact that I was what the Americans call a slacker. I did not want to work hard, nor work smart; in fact, I did not want to work at all. I wanted to slack off and be a ball of nothingness wrapped up in my cocoon of oblivious mediocrity. I was aiming for the title of Kris, Loafer of the Year.

I didn't try to hide any of my shortcomings. Neither did I try to pretend that I was dumber than I was. So reports of my future worthiness would keep coming in. 'Your son has the potential to top his class,' said one teacher to my dad. 'Kris can better fulfil his potential if he applies himself,' said another. But my personal favourite was: 'Kris has the intelligence to be the best.' The best at what? The best me? What the fuck did that even mean? I wasn't one of those idiots who have no idea of what they could be. I knew my own potential. I could be anything I wanted to be, because when it came to the things I loved I really did apply myself. It was only a quirk of fate that the things I loved were comic books, video games and movies.

In India, one does not have much of a future as a comic book writer or a video game developer or even a movie star. 'Hold on to that last thought, Kris,' you might say, 'you could be an actor.' But you'd be wrong. For I am one of those chinky-eyed Mongol-origin types who are Indian but look Chinese and simply do not fit the Bollywood mould. How many of my kind have made it big in Bollywood? You won't even have five names that spring to mind. I'd probably be typecast as the bloody darwaan. Since my dreams were dashed from the beginning, I wanted to simply pass through life without troubling myself or others.

Now, being a slacker shouldn't be such a bad thing. But, in a country where you have to compete with a billion others for everything in life, it is a very bad thing and frowned upon by one and all. We're probably the only people in the world who compete to be mediocre and pounce with drooling mouths on average jobs with average salaries. This probably also explains the humungous number of Indian taxi drivers in New York.

Beware, fellow slackers. At some point, people will stop asking you what you want to be and start telling you what to be. As the end of school drew closer, my 'well-wishers'—read, family, teachers, blah blah blah—told me to join the government services because of the perks and the under-the-table cash. Mostly, I smiled and day-dreamt while they tried to sell me the idea of Kris, the High-flying Government Babu. They said I had the potential to be at the centre of power, but I was not really listening. Anyone can be the best at being corrupt, lazy and pot-bellied—there's simply no challenge in it.

After I finished with school and the prospect of college and freedom loomed large, the questions of career and work became even more pertinent. So I decided to ignore them as much as possible. After all, freedom was almost in my grasp. No more parents nagging at me, no more well-meaning teachers trying to drive me to success and, best of all, no more get-home-quick curfews. I could now smoke with impunity the herb of my choice, drink with gusto the liquid of my preference and grow my hair out to a length that would make my parents cringe. I would be master and commander of my own life for the very first time, and for this I had to prepare.

In order to leave home, one must go to college away from home. Hence my aim was to get into one far, far away. Now, choosing a college down in the plains is no small task. Most students will try to get into the best college possible. They'll read the websites and check if they like the course material, they'll go through the list of teaching faculty to aid their quest for academic success. I skipped those steps altogether and settled on the city of Kolkata, a metropolis renowned for its intelligence, culture and, most importantly, the night life which ended at five in the morning while every other city shut down its clubs and went home by midnight. However, the main reason was that my girlfriend of the last two years was also in Kolkata. Basically, while almost everyone I knew was going to college to gain knowledge and improve their prospects, I was going to get away from home and get laid. What can I say? I was horny and a virgin at seventeen, which is not a good combination.

After a lot of haggling, with blessings for my scholarly endeavours from my parents, I bid farewell to the land of my birth, the cold mountains of North Bengal, and said hello to the sweltering summer heat of Kolkata. When the train pulled into the station at Sealdah, after a sweaty night's journey, to deposit me on the platform, the first thing I noticed was how hot the damned place was; the second was how sticky it could get. To a hillbilly like me, Kolkata felt like an invisible person was rubbing greasy chewing gum into my skin every five minutes. I took about twelve baths every day in my first year of college, that's how damned hot it was.

I lay panting at the station that day, dazzled by the odorous populace of working-class Kolkata, until my cousin came and picked me up. Tyson—or Cousin Ty, as we called him—was a Kolkata veteran. The bugger had been studying there for the last five years and was now working for some big-time MNC. Everyone in the family would yammer about how well he was doing and how they had never expected it from him and so on and so forth. However, he looked to me like some kind of junkie, or maybe a zombie. Bleary-eyed and visibly pissed, he looked worse off than me.

Cousin Ty was short, a little tanned, talked a lot. Usually, he made a great impression on everyone he met—unlike me, who left people with the impression that 'This boy is very weird'. If I was the black sheep of the family, Ty was the golden boy who made everyone happy. However, we got along—always had—so this was not the reunion I was expecting. No hugs, no fond abuses, just a sleepy cousin greeting me grumpily. With grunts and a few rude hand gestures, he guided me through the mass of humanity at Sealdah station. Sitting in a yellow decaying Kolkata taxi, he lit a smoke and offered me one. In between drags of his cigarette, he gave me a short tour of Kolkata while directing the taxi to Tollygunge, which is where he stayed and where I too would reside for the next few years of my life.

As I gazed out of the taxi window at the sights and sounds of the City of Joy, I observed how Kolkatans went about their daily business. It was rush hour and the entire city was out in full force. Car horns blared and drivers offered the choicest abuses, oscillating between those of the maternal and those of the sisterly variety. Yet, wonder of wonders, not a finger was lifted in violence. Nor was there a drop of bloodshed. I wondered out loud how Kolkatans could stay so calm in the face of so much chaos and colourful bad-mouthing.

'They are all gentlemen.' Ty yawned. 'This is how civilized people behave. They abuse people, but they don't fight.'

This really bothered me. Either the average Bengali male had water in his veins or they all really were that civilized and cultured. Where I came from, people fought at the drop of a hat. A sneer or a gaze that lingered too long would result in knuckle sandwiches all around.

By the time we reached Ty's flat, I was drenched in sweat and feeling like a wet noodle. An education was the farthest thing from my mind and my initial desire to get laid had been dulled by the incredible human momo-steamer that was Kolkata. I felt like I had died and gone to the sauna from hell and was regretting not choosing a nice hill station college to study in. I felt a lot better after a cold bath, but that lasted all of thirty minutes. It amazed me how people got anything done in the heat. I wondered if offices, colleges and schools had air conditioners installed.

Somehow I managed to get admitted to a college and even got laid in that maddening heat. After that, I spent three years doing not much at all in Kolkata. I got stoned. I got civilized like the Bengalis, no longer picking fights at every provocation. I learnt the fine art of haggling and the finer art of the evening siesta. I grew my hair long, toasted the memory of my lost virginity with copious sex, drank, smoked and partied with impunity any day of the week and twice on Sundays. I even made Bengali friends.

I learnt to love the old city with its intellectuals and faux intellectuals. The Chinese food which tasted too spicy and sweet became my staple diet and the language which had once been just a gabble to my ears became yet another tongue which I spoke badly. I was well on my way to becoming a Kolkatan, in that strange place which resisted all change. My dad, when he visited me, called Kolkata a time machine. Apparently, some things from the 1970s were still the same even in the new century.

In between all that, one question still niggled and poked at my subconscious: Kris, what do you want to be? I still did not have a friggin' clue. My life was complete and perfect in its laidback laziness. But, as with all good things, this too had to come to an end. Nothing, as the song goes, lasts forever. In the summer of 2006, I became a graduate with marks that left me neither here nor there. I tried not to be bothered still, but life was finally catching up. My darling parents decided to drop a bomb on me.

'Either you come back home and prepare for the government exams, or you get a job,' said Mother Dearest. In a way, it was ever so modern of them—they were probably banking on my inherent laziness to propel me home and towards a job with the Government of India. So it was a great surprise to them when I declared confidently, 'Okay, then, I'm going to go get a job.'

There was silence on the other end of the phone and for a while I thought that Mom had fainted. 'Let me know when you find something,' she said finally, and somehow, even though I could not see her, I had the eerie feeling that she had on her face a sadistic smile that stretched from ear to ear.

After such an incredible life-changing decision, I felt euphoric and depressed at the same time. To work and to earn meant I would have to suffer and toil. But, on the other hand, the idea of living under my parents' roof and following their rules was pure anathema. So I had to pull up my socks, garters and whatever else I could and go get a job in the name of freedom. The alternative was unthinkable.

Like every young go-getting Indian, I consulted my peers and took the advice of my elders before embarking on a job hunt of any kind. However, since my peers were stoners and good-for-nothings and my elders comprised biryani sellers and hash dealers, I kind of figured their advice would suck very badly. The only person who seemed to have any kind of grip on reality and good advice to offer was Bidisha.

Here we shall take a moment to admire the fine qualities of my girlfriend back then. Today, we might be distant strangers; but when we were together, she was painted my world in Eastman colours and was my Rock of Gibraltar. She was smart, intelligent, driven and courageous to a fault. The very things that made me love her back then became the reasons I couldn't stand her later. She was a year older, a foot shorter and a whole lot crazier than me. And she was an absolute tigress in bed. Which is probably why I did not notice her other qualities till much later.

Anyhow, Bipasha had been working in the same call centre as Ty for the last year, where her campaign or process sold pizzas and colas to Americans. She called it a BPO, a business process outsource; I told her she worked for a pizza place. They got paid well, though, because in this city there were very few jobs that pay well and sometimes there are jobs that do not pay at all. Kolkata was the cheapest metropolis in the country; alongside, it was also the lowest paying one.

Once I had scanned the list of options available, I decided that I too should give the call centre market a try. Cousin Ty put in his two cents as well and thoroughly endorsed the open work culture, the great up-scaling opportunities and the learning experience. Basically, he tried to sell me the whole concept, band baaja baraat included. I am not easily led into any decisions, especially when there is work involved. But Bidisha and Ty together made a very strong case, even if I did have to work a night shift. Anyway, it was something I was used to. I hardly slept at night. Plus, I need not wear formal clothes all the time and I could keep my long hair. That made up my mind for me.

Ty and Bidisha gave me referrals and lined up a list of interviews. I put my CV on some job sites as well and sat back, waiting for an interview call. My friends from college were also doing the same. Most of them wanted to study further; but some, like me, wanted to work, they wanted to take a break from studies and see what was out there. The only thing that separated me from everyone else was that they had a purpose and I was simply avoiding choosing a path.

Things would have been easier if there had been a path that I wanted to take. Now, somewhat older and wiser, I can say firmly that having a path or a goal that you believe in makes you all the more likely to succeed at it. I did, I suppose have a path of sorts, but it was a regressive one—I was employing all my energies in avoiding a real career. Cousin Ty will probably get angry if he reads this. As will many other call centre workers, for they will argue that their work makes for real careers too. But it's their career, not mine, and real to them, not to me. If I could have figured out what I wanted to do in life early on, it would have saved me many sleepless nights, both literally and figuratively.

As the cliché goes, you only know how much a person is worth once you lose them. While they're around, the tendency to take people for granted is immense. Where am I going with this, you ask? Well, I am going where every boy or girl has gone before: heartbreak hotel. The state of being where you lament the loss of your beloved.

Bidisha was ambitious. And she thought that the world of the BPO held many possibilities. Unknown to me, she was letting her ambitions run full throttle and flirting wholesale with her team leader. Ty, I found out, had known about this, but he'd dismissed it as office politics, wherein Bidisha was using her feminine wiles to get things done. I, on the other hand, am not an ambitious person. Bidisha considered this a fatal flaw. My indolence, lethargy and overall lack of drive had been bothering her. It was the age-old story in which a woman chose to be comfortable, rich and bored rather than in love and struggling to make ends meet. It takes a rare woman to choose to join her destiny with that of someone like me, a man who is going nowhere. I really didn't blame her. Wait. On second thoughts, it was all her bloody fault.

Bidisha could have said all this to my face and dumped me in a graceful manner. Instead, I had to find out from friends that something fishy was going on between Bidisha and her team leader. The whole idea of being betrayed pissed me off to a spectacular extent. I had to get answers, so I took a taxi straight to her office, where they were having a team party that day. I called Bidisha and asked her to meet me downstairs in the lobby. She stalled for time and told me she could not meet me till the entire team had eaten dinner. I told her I would wait. As I fumed and raged at a small coffee joint, it all began to make sense... Her coming home late, her trips to the beaches with her 'team', the phone calls she walked out of the house to answer.

I must have waited at least two hours for her godforsaken team to finish stuffing their faces when I called her again and said, 'Listen, either you come down or I come up and crash your team party.' She begged me not to make a scene and promised she would be down within ten minutes. And she did come down, swaying a little bit in her high heels and her little black dress, smelling of alcohol and smoke, looking lost. Her team leader followed close behind. I was not particularly surprised to see him. I had questions—and the bastard could answer them just as well if she was too drunk to.

'Are you guys seeing each other?' I asked.

'Yes,' said the shmuck.

'How long has this been going on?'

'A while now...'

'Are you sleeping with each other?'

'Do you want the truth?'

I shrugged, praying desperately that he'd say no.

'Yes, we've been sleeping together.'

And my world came crashing down around me.

I know that the macho thing would have been to create a scene. Start a fight, kick his ass, maybe hers too. But at that moment, I felt utterly exhausted, as if I had run a marathon with someone riding piggyback. I felt stoned, trapped in the worst kind of trip, numb. Even crying or saying something seemed like too much of an effort. I drifted slowly out of the office, got into a taxi and went home.

I walked wordlessly past Ty who was watching TV like a zombie, oblivious to what had just happened. I sat on my bed and lit a smoke. I smoked cigarette after cigarette, as if the nicotine and the smoke could somehow erase what had just happened. I had really loved Bidisha. I had wanted to marry her. But she had betrayed me, cheated on me, made me feel like killing myself. I cried, and the hot tears came faster and faster, as if someone had turned on a tap to drain a long-forgotten tank.

I cried myself to sleep for the next two weeks. I spoke to no one, ate little, smoked a lot of pot. I watched TV and cried while watching sappy Hindi movies. I listened to songs on my iPod and cried when something reminded me of her. In the meantime, Bidisha came to the house and took away all her clothes and things. I felt blank as I stared at the empty spaces where her things had used to be. An endless loop of memories played in my head, I was drowning in sadness fuelled by weed and despair. I was really wallowing in it, and I suspected faintly that I might secretly be enjoying it.

Then, finally, Ty walked into my room. 'Listen, I know this is tough, but you're better off without the bitch. Now get off your fucking ass and do something.'

I lay on my stomach, with my face buried in the pillow, and pretended that Ty hadn't said anything, that the world did not exist. But he was right. I could not mope forever. Besides, there was a silver lining to all this. I was now single and ready to mingle.

It was not such a disaster after all. I was still young, reasonably good-looking and smart, even if I was a little aimless. I needed to work and get her off my mind. So I buckled up and got ready to face the world again. I had narrowly averted depression and turning into the stoners' equivalent of Devdas.

From this episode in my life, I told myself, I had gained an insight into the inner workings of a woman's mind. Actually, it still remained a mystery to me—the only thing I had really gained was a healthy wariness for the opposite sex. In addition, I now hated all Anglo-Indians—the team-leader-cum-new-boyfriend was an Anglo. I also hated in no particular order call centres, my ex and life in general. To top it all, I still had to get a job, else I would have to go back to my parents. The job situation was now like a rotten tooth—I knew it had to be pulled, yet I kept avoiding it. But then my mother's voice on the phone, declaring that she was going to cut off my funding in a week, spurred me into action.

2

BIG BLUE

Awe-inspiring is not exactly a term used to describe call centres, but that's how it was for me on so many levels. The call for my interview came in response to a Horrorjob.com application made about a month before and, well, beggars cannot be choosers. So it came to pass that after having sworn to never again enter the portals of a call centre, I arrived at Gate No. 5 of Big Blue Enterprises one Monday morning. Cousin Ty, who'd come to drop me off with advice on what to say at the interview, waved me good luck. He seemed pleased that I was finally getting off my depressed butt.

I sauntered in and was ushered towards a waiting area by an aunty-type woman who looked at me quite sadly, as if I were a young goat to be presently slaughtered halaal style. I was an hour late, and already crammed in the small area were men and women dressed in formals, all determined to join the workforce of Big Blue. With a pounding hangover and stinking of smoke—only some of it was tobacco smoke—I was supremely underdressed in my collared T-shirt and jeans. But who gave a damn? I ignored the men and discreetly leered at the women. A gay-looking-sounding-and-acting HR guy collected hastily typed CVs from everyone, including me—mine was probably the hastiest typed.

Before the interviews, began we were fed copious amounts of brainwashing dialogue by a slightly plump but pretty Punjabi recruiter, whose big tits jiggled under her corporate power suit as she spoke excitedly about what an opportunity we were getting, what our future prospects were going to be and how we would fast rise up the corporate ladder like dough on super-yeast. The office lighting and various propaganda posters declaring what a great place Big Blue was to work at reminded me just a bit of the Nazis and a little bit of Bollywood trailers.

The whole interview experience kind of felt like I had smoked something that had gone bad and was giving me a rotten trip. But, what can I say? I needed the money, they needed a phone jockey and it was a beautiful meeting of two hearts, like them Laila met Majnu type deals, like Adam met Eve and... Hold on, that pile of horse manure didn't exactly work out that great, did it?

Five hours later, after clearing round after round of mind-numbing interviews with managers and assessors from every ass-monkey department they had, I was finally selected to work for Big Blue as a technical support agent (whatever the fuck that was). The less unfortunate slunk back into whatever holes they had crawled out from—to the victor went the spoils.

The filling of employment forms, photocopying of documents, sticking of passport-size photographs and signing of contracts in intricate triplicate still awaited me. Throughout this brain-warping exercise, during which every inane question was answered smartly by yours truly, not once did I spy a nice-looking chick, not even one decent looker, just bloody homely types. Where do the hot women hide in India?

Upon finally, finally submitting the applications, we each received the terms of our contract and promises of salaries to be earned. Tired but hopeful, I dragged myself homewards, just a little starry-eyed and dazzled by the corporate magnificence that was Big Blue. On the return bus journey back to our rat hole of a flat, while being assaulted by the unwashed, deodorant-free armpits of the Indian populace, I remember feeling distinctly pleased that I had a job with a multinational company, even if it was a call centre.

It was October, which meant that everyone was gearing up for Durga puja. But I didn't feel much like celebrating. In Kolkata, the puja celebrations are quite elaborate and pandal-hopping is an activity that ranks much higher on the social calendar than pub-hopping. I had been avoiding the whole festival for the last three years, but this time I was stuck, in the middle of that bus. Everyone except me looked happy and dressed up, and I felt myself torn between hatred and envy about this. I stared down at my shiny new ID card with my face plastered on it and I realized that I was now a part of corporate India. The feeling made me want to throw up and at the same time hang the card around my neck to proudly declare that I was a Big Blue employee. It was strange mix of pride and disgust, and I didn't know whether I wanted to go home and celebrate with Ty or just get off the bus and hurl myself under the wheels.

What eventually tipped the scales in Big Blue's favour was that as soon as I had been initiated and made an employee, I had also been given my bank paperwork. I now had an ATM card all of my own and an account in a bank that would promptly fill up with money on the first day of every month. I promised myself that I would save my money, and the feeling of being independent and an earning, tax-paying Indian citizen made my chest swell with pride.

When I reached home, Ty congratulated me. The look on his face seemed to say: 'My boy is finally growing up.' I found out on Facebook that my ex had moved in with her team leader and they were now living together. This depressed me so much that I promptly smoked two joints, ate dinner and went to bed despite the loudspeakers blaring their devotional music at eleven in the night. My last thought before sleep took hold of me was: whatever else might be fucked up about my life, I finally had a job—I was going to be self-sufficient, no longer under my parents' thumbs.

It was only later, much later, that I realized that taking calls for a living is frowned upon in India. The funny stares I got from people when I told them I worked at a call centre made me feel like maybe I would have been better off shovelling some ripe cowdung.

3

THE HONEYMOON PHASE

For the edification of those who have not had the incredible, once-in-a-lifetime opportunity of taking calls for a living, this is how they prepare you. It's a three-month training period, fondly called the 'honeymoon period', because once you hit the floor you really get buggered. They put you in a temporary team and give you targets for sales and other wonderful activities because dhanda hai, nothing's for free, and other motivating causes come into play. Then you finally get shoved into a more or less permanent team with a team leader. Voila! You are now a 'chor-porate' employee.

Training at a call centre is a funny sort of process. They teach you all manners of things that make you believe that you are about to perform the most important task in the world, that is, taking calls. They tell you about things like customer service and how it is so fucking important to make sure that you are ethical at all times. But the moment you hit the production floor, all that talk becomes a happy memory. Have you ever told a white lie to get something? Well, we told lots of white lies. We still do. If it gets the job done, then so be it.

The nicest part about working for a call centre is the pickup and drop home. No longer did I have to endure the odoriferous armpits and cheap perfumes of public transport. It was a small blessing in light of the horrors we were soon to endure. The first month for trainees is mostly spent learning how to 'oooh' and 'aaah' in English, supervised by a trainer who looks very Indian but speaks such crisp English that you would be forgiven for thinking the British left him behind. Then again, not all trainers are created equal—or, as my grandmother liked to say, 'All fingers on your hand are not the same length.'

And so it was that our Bengali babu trainer, who was half rock star, half Lothario and all-round jackass, came to train us. There were thirty or so of us huddled into a training room where he breezed in looking like a biker gang reject. His bloodshot eyes and incessant scratching indicated clearly that he was on some variant of Speed. Now, any pill that gets you up and going qualifies as Speed. Usually, in Kolkata, the pharmacies are more than happy to hand you some Spaz or N 10 or cough syrup, the classic favourite of junkies everywhere. Our trainer Shantanu was definitely high as a kite and none too happy to be at work.

I was customarily late for the voice and accent training, despite being picked up for work from home. After being suitably reprimanded for my lateness and unprofessionalism by a short, stubby and grumpy trainer, I seated my royal behind right at the back of the training room. Later, I found out that her name was Riya Ganguly, and so Grumpy Ganguly we shall henceforth call her.

Once I'd made myself comfortable, conversation ensued with the other trainees. Where are you from? What did you do before this? Etc., etc. And then she walked in, like a summer breeze, noticing everyone and yet no one. She had that subtle kind of smile that said someone had told her a fantastic joke and made her laugh, and you bloody well wished you were that someone. With her slit eyes and beautifully high cheekbones, she was clearly from the northeast. So, yes, she was pretty, and she was ignoring me. She was ignoring everyone, including the bloody jackass of a trainer. The situation made me wish I could pull some eyeball-grabbing stunt. Like a 180-degree leg split across two running motorbikes. Or, at the very least, bend some iron bars while promising to drink some canine blood. She definitely got my blood running. I was hooked at first sight.

And did mention that she had a body to die for? Skin so pale that it looked like marble. And curves that reminded me of ripe tropical fruit. Ordinarily, I would have fallen head over heels in love for her. But I had recently been cured of that affliction. Love was just a jumble of emotions born from hormones acting on the brain—in much the same manner as cocaine, which is a fact supported by science. I was immune, I told myself, and her kryptonite could no longer affect me.

My gentle musings on ripe mangoes were rudely interrupted by Shantanu babu, who wanted a round of introductions. But the jackass—we shall henceforth refer to him as Jackass—decided to put his own spin on it. We all had to sing after introducing ourselves. Some sang well, most sang badly. I too sang, a little off-key, after stating my name, rank and serial number.

Then it was time for Miss Tropical Fruit to introduce herself. I had barely caught her very complicated name when she began to sing. She sang some lame song, but it sounded like the bloody angels themselves had descended from heaven and decided to harmonize. Needless to say, I was blown away. A quick glance around the room told me that everyone else was also in the same condition. Jackass's face bore the look of a hungry jackal who has spied a lame hen. I could tell that there was going to be bad blood between him and me when Jackass decided to join his voice to Miss Tropical Fruit's, turning the song into a duet. I felt like running the idiot down with a car.

After that, Jackass followed up with more dialogue and brainwashing about the opportunities at Big Blue, all the while flashing his pearly whites at the class in general and Miss Tropical Fruit in particular. He explained how he was now about to take up the incredible task of teaching us village bumpkins to speak English as it was meant to be spoken. From correcting how we pronounced words to how we constructed sentences, this chap was going to do it all—and in the process, I gathered, bore us to death.

Upon noticing that I was yawning, Jackass fixed me with a deathly stare. 'You! What is your name?'

'Um, me? My name is Kris.'

'Why are you yawning?'

'I'm sleepy.'

'Did you not sleep at home?'

'Uh, no, my girlfriend kept me awake all night.' An awkward silence followed. 'She was not feeling well,' I added finally.

Yes, Bidisha did keep me up all night—rather, her memories did. I was about to pitch into gloom again when Miss Tropical Fruit gave me a smile that lit me right up and all my dark thoughts were dispelled. I could tell she was one of those females who like their men to be all romantic and cheesy. However, Jackass was not impressed. He hauled me to the front of the room and gave me a topic to speak on: 'Are live-in relationships destroying Indian values?'

As I scoured my brains to deliver the tongue-lashing that he so justly deserved, Grumpy Ganguly interrupted, saving Jackass (and everyone else) from my glowing wit.

'Jackass, let's go. It's time for our meeting.'

'I'll be right back,' growled Jackass as he left the room.

While most of my batch mates were aghast at what they saw as my lack of respect for authority, a few decided that I was buddy material. I made friends immediately.

Stan—Stanley, an Anglo from Picnic Garden—had, like me, just finished college. He liked to get stoned and then sit for training. Apparently, it was the only thing that made the whole experience bearable. The weed helped him concentrate—but on what he had no idea. This job was just a stop-gap till he started his course in software engineering. He was a short, pleasant fellow and had some pot on him all the time.

Wribhu—pronounced Reevu—was half Nepali and half Bengali. He liked to smoke a lot and drink a lot. He also liked to fight after getting drunk, as we found out when we all went out drinking. But when he wasn't fighting, he was just really nice guy who couldn't decide whether he was Bengali or Nepali.

Dibyajyoti had worked at quite a few call centres and knew his way around. He was the career BPO employee and he was sure that this 'golden opportunity' at Big Blue would get him places. A bit senior to us, he was the dada of the group and liked to dominate the adda.

The others really didn't appreciate my smart-aleck replies in class or my laidback attitude. Perhaps they thought I was getting ahead of myself. I really couldn't care. I had Stan, Wribhu and Dibya to keep me company on my smoke breaks; the rest could take a dive off their lemming-conformist boards.

In the next four weeks of training, we discovered that there were many more such 'meetings' that Grumpy, Jackass and some others of their tribe would go for. They would constantly take smoke breaks, thus giving us much-needed intervals from all their bullshit. I took my breaks with the others, but noticed only Miss Tropical Fruit. Her name was Imsen Hangsing, I found out. Eventually, we got to know each other a little better. She was from a state in the northeast, as I had figured. She was engaged to be married in a year and, before that, she wanted to live in the big city for a while. She was simple yet beautiful, a little shy yet bolder than most girls. The best part was that she lived in the same area as me. So we got picked up by the same company cab together and dropped home together as well, which gave us some time to talk to each other. And I swear to God that in all that time I did not have a single indecent thought about her. Okay, maybe one or two.

Training went by in a haze of phonetics, grammar and training games. Then, one day, Jackass gleefully announced that our mock calls were approaching. A mock call is a controlled-environment call that you get marked on. You follow a script and improvise as well, and if you make the cut than you graduate to more training—else it's tata–goodbye, as they say in Kolkata.

The sheer nervous energy in a room full of trainees about to take a mock call is incredible. Especially when your trainer is a nutcase, high as a kite and out to make you look like a moron. Upon discovering that Imsen would not give in to his sleazy advances, Jackass had taken to plaguing me. He tried to quiz me on grammar, on articles, nouns, pronouns and verbs. It was pretty hilarious seeing him try to trip me up. After failing with me, he usually took out his frustration on everyone else in class, which was not pretty to watch.

'Introduce yourself,' he yelled at a guy one day.

'Myself Manoj, I studied in the Uneebarsheety of Burdwan.'

Okay, so maybe it wasn't pretty to watch—or hear—because most Indians have a really bad grasp on English grammar and pronunciation. It's not really their fault, though—it's pretty much what they have been taught. However, there were exceptions to this rule, and some smartasses caught on real quick. Every once in a while, you got really angry and abusive customers out to make your ears bleed. Here's what one smart aleck did to even the score during one of his calls.

'Thank you for calling Big Blue technical support. May I have your first and last name please?'

'Fuck you.'

'Okay, sir, your first name is Fuck and your last name is You. Can I call you by your first name, Fuck?'

It was a pity they had to fire Smart Aleck after that little stunt, because I could tell that he would have really livened up the office with his wit. The bosses had to make an example, though, because you can sell crap to the customer, you can lie your buttocks off, you can pull every sneaky, underhanded trick in the book, but never, never-ever-ever, can the humble Indian call centre worker ever abuse his customer.

4

GETTING TRAINED

The most elementary skill one must possess at a call centre is the ability to speak English correctly. You must not only understand the customer but also endeavour to make yourself understood. In order to do this, you must learn to speak English right from the basic building blocks. This, in short, meant that Jackass was going to drive us stark raving nuts, utterly and completely bonkers, trying to correct miniscule flaws in our pronunciation.

Every morning would begin with songs to perk us up—or, as most of us suspected, to perk Shantanu up. He started looking progressively worse as the training wore on. I guess he must have been upping his dosage of pills and getting higher than ever. It was a miracle that he even managed to stand in class, let alone train us without drooling on the projector. This might have been in part due to Imsen not paying attention to his lame one-liners. Or maybe this was just how he was. The strange thing was that the rest of the class, apart from Stan, Wribhu, Dibya and me, did not seem to notice that our trainer was high. However, the drilling of sounds—vowel, consonant and diphthong—would continue to assail us no matter how wasted Jackass looked.

His formula for better English was 'ah ah ee ee oo oo ay ay' repeated ad nauseum every day for better vowel sounds to better emote our words. 'Puh puh puh, kuh kuh kuh, tuh tuh tuh', we had to say over and over again to better pronounce our consonants. If we didn't match up to his standards, he would rant at us. Strangely enough, some of it did make sense. Some of my fellow trainees did start speaking a little better, making me think that Jackass was not as full of cow manure as he acted. However, it could also have been that the weed I was smoking with Stan was making me see and hear things.

One major problem with many Indians is that they speak English like they speak their mother tongue. One chap at Big Blue apparently asked his team leader for a holiday, saying: 'I need a holiday as I need to go to the village to sell my land along with my wife.' Now, the veracity of that story is a bit suspect since Jackass was the one telling it, but you get the general idea. The Big B once said in a movie that he talked English, he walked English—in order to speak the language properly, you must take his example and also think English.

After the unending lessons in grammar and drills in sounds and word pronunciation, we hapless trainees had to endure sessions of games and activities designed to make us 'better employees'. At the end of it, we were all pretty sick of the whole thing. But since Wribhu, Dibya and Stan would sit stoned in class, they acted as if everything, including the grammar tests, was a fun activity. The only saving grace was that we got to sing every day in our horrendous voices, and Imsen sang with us, making everything better all at once.

The only real break in the monotony of training was that every once in a while they would let us watch a movie they said was related to training. Now, I understand how *My Fair Lady* qualified, but how on earth does *Finding Nemo* help us speak better English or feel more motivated? Jackass sure had some strange ideas about how to train us. But we weren't complaining. After all, we were getting paid to sit in class and repeat his nonsense. The icing on the cake was that we still had two more months of very similar training to finish.

We also had sessions in between classes when the training manager, Miss Rita Daryanani, would check up on us. She would have nice friendly chats with us, asking how training was going and what they could do to make our lives easier. In this way, she was also collecting feedback on Jackass. The whole system of checks and balances seemed damned professional to me. I was very impressed by the whole order and logic of it all.

The days inched closer to our final mock calls, which would determine whether we moved into process and technical training. While some of us practised our call scripts and took things easy, the weaker trainees started panicking like Armageddon was upon them. Jackass started showing signs of stress as well. His job performance ratings and incentives all depended on how well we did at the mock calls. In hindsight, he was not such a bad chap overall, maybe just a tad too eager to go after the ladies. But he did a fairly good job of training those with weak English.

Imsen and I kept up our friendly banter, spending more time in each other's company. Every now and then, I would feel a little guilty because she did have a fiancé back home, but I never felt like I was doing anything really wrong.

In the meantime, the mock calls were turning into a real task for most of the class. People were failing miserably at not just holding a make-believe conversation with Shantanu but also at following the call script. How hard is it to follow a call script? You memorize the opening and improvise on the conversation. It is easy to tell when a customer is angry, sad, anxious, or in a real hurry. Empathizing and being genuinely concerned is a simple task, but you need a firm grasp over English to make it happen. One of the more horrid mock calls went like this.

Trainee: 'Sir, you sound very tired. Is everything all right?'

Shantanu (standing in for the customer): 'Well, my mother just passed away. I had to pay a lot for her funeral, which just got over. I am tired and I just want to fix my computer to send some mail.'

Trainee: 'I am very sorry for your loss, sir. Where was she last laid?'

Now that was a line that definitely killed me. No one had any idea what the fuck he was going on about. How can you ask a customer about his dead mother's last sexual encounter? However, it turned out that the trainee wanted to know where she was last laid to rest—buried, that is.

Sometimes Shantanu would also play the fool, deliberately confusing the trainees' instructions to repair a computer. If a trainee asked him to 'shut Windows', he would go around closing pretend windows and then ask if he needed to close the doors as well. This got him a lot of laughs and also drove home the message that all American customers might not be dumb as bricks but most of them would be pretty thick. In fact, during my calling tenure, I encountered a customer who wanted to know how the beer mug holder on his laptop could be fixed. I was absolutely stumped until I figured out that he had been using the DVD tray to keep his beer.

The last week of training was crazier than all the rest put together because we would have our final voice and accent mock calls. Imsen wanted to practice with me and so we did whenever we had the time. After class one day, as our car pool was dropping us home, Imsen asked me if I wanted to practise some more.

'Sure, why not?' I said.

We agreed to go to her flat and practise our mock calls. I was hungry when we got off the cab, so we picked up some fried rice from a local joint. We got on a rickshaw and chatted as we made our way to her flat. She told me that she lived with her cousin who had gone to visit her friends. I was feeling nervous about being alone with her in her flat. Nothing was going to happen, I told myself again and again.

Imsen served me the fried rice on a plate and I ate while she changed in the other room. Funnily enough, my hunger had somewhat disappeared. I looked around. It was a tidy little room. Her bed was neatly made and had a poster of her favourite singer looming large next to it. The fan overhead spun lazily. I shivered a little as Imsen returned to the room and sat down next to me.

I think we practised our mock calls and then talked about work and life in general for quite a bit, but I really can't remember much. It was getting late and I needed to go home, but I couldn't bring myself to leave. I was searching for an excuse to leave when I noticed a guitar lying in a corner. I asked her if she played. Wordlessly, she went over, picked up the guitar and started playing it. She sang a song in Kuki, her mother tongue, to go with the tune, and I could almost feel myself falling for her. I must have looked like a right idiot as I gaped at her. When the music stopped, I walked over to her.

Imsen let the guitar rest and smiled at me. 'Now it's time for you to go home.'

'What if I don't want to?'

'We have mock calls tomorrow. You need to sleep. There's always a next time.'

On the rickshaw home, in between all the bumping and jostling of the Kolkata lanes, I wondered what she'd meant when she said that there is always a next time. I slept fitfully that night, and the next day in the pickup Imsen sat in front, absolutely silent. I was wondering if I had offended her in some way when my cell phone buzzed.

'Good luck today. Imsen,' said the text.

I texted her back with a smile on my face. 'Good luck to you too.' The smile grew bigger as I realized that I now had her number. God alone knows where she got my number from.

Shantanu was strangely subdued as he wished us all luck while warning the weaker ones about the mistakes they could make. Grumpy Ganguly was going to take our mock calls and the lead trainer, Anju Reddy, a stern-looking South Indian lady, would also be present.

One by one we entered the room where we were supposed to take our final mock calls. While everyone was still practising, I was wondering what it would be like to kiss Imsen. I was all wrapped up in my little fantasy when someone tapped my shoulder. It was Shantanu.

'Kris, you have a lot of potential. Do well in the mock calls. You can become a trainer someday, so don't waste your opportunities.'

I was pleasantly surprised. After all, it had been a while since anyone had told me I had any potential for anything. Plus, the fact that Shantanu had said it made it more special since I knew he hated my guts and wouldn't say something nice if it weren't true.

When my turn came, I was feeling quite confident. And when Imsen wished me luck and winked at me, I felt like I could reduce mountains to rubble. I walked into the room and sat facing Grumpy Ganguly and Anju Reddy.

'Name and employee number please,' said Grumpy as she typed into her computer.

I answered and noticed that Ms Reddy was looking very intently at me. Now, I'm a pretty good-looking guy, even if I do say so myself, but she was looking just a bit too hard. There is the look that says: 'I am interested in you'. There is the look that says: 'I find you hot'. And then there is the look that says: 'I am going to stalk you and save your toenail clippings'. Guess which look she had on her face? Or maybe I was just being paranoid from all the mock call stress. I sincerely hoped that that was all it was.

Before Grumpy could even begin the mock call, Anju began her own cross-examination. 'Where are you from?' she demanded.

'North Bengal,' said.

'So what is the weather like this time of year?'

'It's almost winter, so it's going to be pretty cold there. Much colder than Kolkata. But the views of the mountains, all covered in snow, are incredible right now.'

I did misjudge her initial interest in me. Turned out that she wanted to know more about my hometown because she was looking to go on a holiday with her family. Grumpy Ganguly in the meantime was staring intently at us. Anju turned to her and said, 'You can skip the mock call for Kris.' I was dismissed.

I was stunned. Could she do that? How exactly would I be graded? Would I pass or be failed? Would I have to suffer the ignominy of retraining?

As I walked out of the room, the other trainees swarmed around me, asking me what exactly had gone down. They were looking for clues to make their own calls easier, but I really did no advice to offer. I told Stan, Wribhu and Dibya what had happened and they told me to take it easy. Dibya laughed and said that this sort of thing happened sometimes.

Imsen came over and sat next to me. I must have been looking upset because she squeezed my hand and said, 'Don't worry. You must have done just fine.' I was so perturbed that it took to me a while to notice that she was holding my hand. I smiled at her. She returned the smile and we sat like that till her turn came.

Imsen came out of the training room in ten minutes or so with a wide smile on her face. 'You'll never guess what just happened!'

'She asked you for holiday trip suggestions?' I said.

'How did you...'

'She did the same thing with me.'

Imsen's smile grew broader and I felt relieved that at least someone else had had the same weird session in place of their mock call.

Imsen and I had some time to kill as the rest of our batch mates went through their calls. We went to the office cafeteria and ordered our food.

'Is this our candlelight dinner?' she asked over mouthfuls of chicken biryani.

I laughed. She had quite an appetite for a girl. I liked that she could eat. Some guys are not comfortable with the idea that women can eat as voraciously as men, but I love it when a girl eats well. It feels much more natural than hanging out with the skinny, size-zero types—and I like curves. Besides, you can tell a lot about a person from the way they eat. Those with raging appetites have very little control over their desires. Those who eat sparingly are control freaks. They who diet are the ones who are never happy with themselves. The snackers and eaters of junk food have no will power and seek their own destruction via a swift heart attack. However, the worst are vegetarians— they might as well become rabbits, because that's what their food habits remind me of.

I deliberately and painstakingly explained my various theories on food to Imsen, who was looking at me like she either wanted to carve my heart out with her fork or she thought I was bonkers. I stopped when I realized that she wasn't saying a word.

'You are a very weird man,' she said finally. 'But I like you.'

I smiled my cheesiest smile, elated at the thought that Imsen liked me.

Just then, Shantanu waved at us from across the cafeteria hall. It was time for the results of our mock call. Those who had passed would now go on to two months of technical and process training. The sad part about all this was not that some of us would have failed the mock call but that the next two months of training would happen at night. Our daytime life as we knew it would be over.

We gathered in the training room and waited for the results to be announced. Shantanu walked in with a look on his face that foreshadowed disaster, especially for the trainees whose livelihoods hinged on getting through training. It might surprise you, but most call centre employees run their households on their salaries. So while most people turn their noses up at such jobs, these guys hanker after them. After, all it's not like there is a wealth of opportunities knocking at the door.

'People, we have a new record of sorts,' Shantanu said with an expression of dire gloom. And then a small smile broke on his face. 'This is the first batch in Big Blue to have 100 per cent conversion!'

We whooped with joy and congratulated each other. We were one step closer to the production floor and making that all-important extra cash. We hurrahed Shantanu and praised him to the high mountains. Yet, he looked somewhat sad, as if being a record-setting trainer was not enough. Later, I found out that Shantanu had been asked to resign. He had apparently overdosed on pills at a recent office party, in full view of the head honchos from Gurgaon. His goose had been cooked well and proper.

I dropped Imsen home that day, but nothing else happened. No music, no enigmatic smiles. I left feeling listless as I considered the possibility that we might just end up being platonic and nothing more. When I reached home, Ty was passed out near his bed, dead drunk after a team party at his office. I left him lying on the floor in a pool of his own puke and went off to sleep.

5

LEARNING SOMETHING

As I dressed for the day—rather, night—at office, Ty's face was decorated by an evil smile, along with his hangover. 'Now you get to see what the night shift is really about,' he gloated ominously. I guess he was a bit mad that I did not clean up his mess, but logic dictates that if you make your bed you have to lie in it too. Ty had made his bed of puke and I let him lie in it. Simple. I headed for the cab to go to work.

My shift would now start at 9.30 p.m. From this day onwards, they would train us on how to do the job we had been hired for. We would learn useful technical skills to fix customers' computers, to guide them on how to perform certain tasks, to chat them up and get their credit card information. It was as exciting as watching houseflies mate—and that's exactly how I feel about it even today. The cab for my pickup came around 7 p.m., a full two hours before I needed to leave in order to get to work on time. I felt like abusing the assholes who made our rosters for the pickup. It hardly made sense to me that they would designate the person who lives farthest off as the first pickup, since he was also the last person to get dropped and so the last to get off the damned cab. But I didn't complain. It got cold in Kolkata around November, so I was grateful that I didn't have to travel by public transport. It wasn't so bad for a hill boy like me, but born and bred Kolkatans had started to look like they were expecting a snowstorm.

I saw a uniformed guard sitting in the front seat with the driver, huddling in his woollen jacket yet making it a point to show off his uniform. This was a new one. One of the older employees in the cab told me that the guard was there because of a very grim reason: a female employee from a large multinational like ours had been found raped and murdered in Pune just the night before. The management had attributed this to a lack of security and upped the manpower, making sure every cab now had a guard. However, since the driver and his helper were the ones who had committed the crime in Pune, I wondered if other security measures would be better instead of having a uniformed showpiece.

I sat bleary-eyed and dozing slightly as the vehicle made its way to people's houses, picking up employees who had the same shift timing as us. The men would delay the vehicle by having a last smoke and the women would delay us by applying the finishing touches on their make-up. Imsen, however, was always on time—which was something I really liked about her. On that first day of technical training, thanks to the empty roads, we reached office an hour early. This gave me and Imsen a few extra moments to hang out and talk.

We sat at one of the makeshift tea stalls that dotted the outside of Big Blue and drank tea while I thought of a good way to ask her out on a date. While I was trying to come up with something stupendously impressive, Imsen said, 'Hey, Kris, do you eat chicken?'

'Yes, sure,' I said.

Imsen smiled and said, 'Then that's what we'll eat on our next weekly off. Come to my place for Christmas lunch.'

I was pleasantly surprised. Had she read my thoughts? I wondered for a moment if she had psychic powers.

'Why do you look so surprised?' Imsen asked.

I smiled sheepishly. Imsen could render me speechless on most days. I don't mean to brag, but I usually have a lot of skill with the ladies. Imsen, however, simply shut down my arsenal. I was rescued from more embarrassing questions from her by the rest of the batch when they came running towards us.

Everyone else was very excited about the night shift and the technical training, whereas I could only hear in my head Ty's warning of doom. I guess the eagerness was also in part because of the fact that the month was almost over and soon our salaries would be credited to our accounts. Soon, when I remembered that I would be spending quality time with Imsen, I too began to feel a spark of excitement.

Huddled in a training room, with lights glaring at us poor rookies as if we were under interrogation, we sat awaiting our trainer. Imsen sat beside me, fiddling with the computer in front of her, playing Solitaire one moment, drawing on Paint the other. The door swung open and in came a very short man accompanied by a tall, heavyset moustachioed fellow.

The short one bellowed in a voice not quite suited to one built so small: 'My name is Indrajit Chatterjee. You may call me Indrajit or dada, but never sir.' He pointed to the tall chap. 'This is my best trainer, Surya Sen, who will be your trainer for the next two months. I will come and train you in sales and process, but first Surya will be training you on how to do your job.'

'Myself Surya,' said the tall guy. 'Till prebiously I was an agent jast like yew. Now I am the technikal trainer and I weel teech you on how to handle kostomers and solbe their essues.' After the clipped pronunciation and perfect grammar of Shantanu, Surya sounded dreadful. His English left much to be desired and his pronunciation was so horrible that even the bottom performers in voice and accent training looked confident that they could do better than him.

There was, however, a surprise in store for us. Surya was a technical trainer, which meant that he knew more about computers and fixing them than any human being has any right to. He quickly quelled the sniggering and giggling at his pronounced accent with a quick round of questions. 'You dere, bhat is the boot loading sequence?' 'How weel you gate reed of a birus ?' 'Bhat is POST?'

These and other questions of the *Kaun Banega Crorepati* variety had us badly stumped. With each question, we were further convinced that we were going to be massacred once we had to take real calls and deal with real issues. Surya, sensing that we were now suitably in awe of his astronomical levels of computer-related knowledge, now began to speak more confidently.

'I bheel teach yew eberything dat yew need to know. You don't worry, I am here, and you mast learn not jast to solbe questions but to know what es achully wrong.'

This was in truth a very important part of technical training. Aside from knowing how to solve a problem, one also had to know how to find out what the problem was. American customers who called Big Blue or any other technical helpline did so because they either had a whopper of an issue or because they did not know what the problem actually was.

For example, sometimes you can spend hours trying to get someone's wireless network set up, only to discover that they don't have a wireless connection in the first place. Customers often can't distinguish between a computer that has gone bust and one in which the operating system has gone bad. Sometimes they call because they can't switch the computer on, and on further probing you find out they have an electricity outage in the area. So, you see, it wasn't just about knowing what to do.

The technical training took us from operating systems to specific problems. While we learnt how Windows XP, Vista and 7 worked, we also had to learn how to work the registry and use various tactics to get rid of an antivirus. Usually, the class would begin with a quick round of question and answers—and woe betide the fool who had not gone home and recapped what had been taught before this. The training was, however, much lighter than the voice and accent training. Once Surya was done with a topic, he would take time to play games with the class or just talk to us and get to know us better. He would also disappear with the rest of the training team for periodic 'meetings', which term, we suspected, was their code for smoke breaks.

Surya and Indrajit were pretty good buddies too. Sometimes they would both sit in class and conduct question-and-answer rounds just to take someone's trip, which is call centre lingo for basic ragging. Now Indrajit was a complete nutter, but he was also said to be the best in the business when it came to marketing and sales. Even Surya, with his ginormous technical knowhow, bowed to Indrajit's greater experience and wisdom on certain matters. Indrajit was also fond of sprouting profanity-laced philosophy, which did not make him popular with the girls in the class. He would say things like 'If you are getting raped regularly then learn to enjoy it' in reference to an underperformer who was getting daily doses of abuse. Or 'I will show you how men pass blood' while talking about how tough it was going to be to pass sales assessments with him.

Surya and Indrajit made abundantly clear what we had only guessed at: if we did not perform, then we would be fired; and performance was all about sales. If you could not meet sales targets, you were done for. It might seem absurd that a technician had to make sales, but that was how it was. It was like going to a doctor who is supposed to heal you and discovering that his priority is to sell you medicines. What finally convinced us how important sales were to our roles was the fact that without hitting sales targets we would not be getting any incentives at all. So, basically, the real money was in making sales. Some people in production were making enough to buy cars and bikes, which should give you an idea of how much money stood to be earned.

Our primary customers were Americans in the age group of old and too-damn-old-for-computers. Surya and Indrajit explained that younger Americans were more computer savvy and would hardly ever call a technical helpline, much less purchase phone support for their computer problems. So the ones who did call were old folks who had no clue how their computers worked and were easy targets for selling things to.

The job at hand was thus to identify the problem on the phone with the customer, fix the issue and then smooth-talk the customer into trusting you. Everything, from the customer-service tactics of empathy and understanding to the technician's tool of 'Your computer will self-destruct in 10, 9, 8...', was geared towards extracting dollars from the customers. If the customer was difficult and we could not sell anything, then the next best thing was to get him to fill up a survey. The survey was something that earned us brownie points with the management: if the customer was happy with our services, they would fill out a positive survey, grading us a full ten on all parameters; the worst possible score was a one. We got incentives based on the number of positive surveys as well, so it was always a good thing to fix the customer's problem.

Indrajit summed up our real goals while taking calls thus: 'These old Americans, buddha-log old farts, have a typical set of excuses. I just retired, I just had surgery, I am on a pension plan, I do not have enough money. Your job is not to feel bad for these grandmas and grandpas. Be nice and say whatever you want, but make sure that you get the sale. Do NOT take no for an answer. Remember, folks, no mercy.'

Now, a technical process where the technicians were actually salesmen seemed like a recipe for disaster, but who were we to argue? Big Blue had been running this particular strategy for five years and it was now their biggest revenue generator. They had twenty teams with monthly sales targets of $20,000 each. This added up to four lakh dollars in sales—which meant that they were making, approximately, a crore and ninety-two lakh rupees every month. And then when you realize that we were just one out of the nine centres they had in India, you have a clear picture of how much money was at stake. Bigger business is better business, and we were just small cogs in the wheel of the great machinery of corporate greed—so who in their right mind would complain against such success? We accepted that selling was the way to go at Big Blue.

I had, in the meantime, more important things to worry about. More immediate things. With every passing day in training, my Christmas lunch date with Imsen was approaching, and I had no idea what was in store. Were we going to make out? If I kissed her, would she get angry? Did she want to be just friends? All these questions were racing through my mind, along with factoids about operating systems and fundas about sales. Basically, my head was completely muddled.

Also, I figured out that Cousin Ty had been right. The night shift sucked royally. It was bloody hard to stay awake and learn things at two in the morning. The effect of sleeping days and working nights could be seen in how sluggish we were becoming. You might think that our jobs were easy, but guess what? Working night shifts day in and day out makes people go nuts. Add to that the fact that we had to try and sleep in the daytime, when the sun is shining bright, and—voila!—you have a set of call centre zombies.

It was really not an easy job to do, and it was even harder to make progress in. For agents to be promoted, there were not just interviews they had to clear but also data requirements or objectives they had to meet for at least six months. And, in a process like ours, where sales mattered the most, the data hinged on how much was sold every day, week and month. Then we had to clear the interview—there were maybe five positions on offer, for which a hundred or so other agents would appear after clearing a written exam. The promotion interviews were called IJP or Internal Job Postings—we renamed it Internal Jaan Pehchaan. Those who had contacts could always rely on good old-fashioned nepotism to pull them through.

Training was turning into a blur of information and online exams and such. Every week we had a set of exams we had to pass to prove our technical training was not in vain. They were supposed to be heavily monitored; instead, Indrajit or Surya discreetly supplied us with the right answers for quizzes. So, come Monday, which was test time, most of us did very well. Amazingly, enough, even with all this 'help' some people managed to fail again and again.

Why were Surya and Indrajit helping us cheat, you might ask. The deal here was that the trainers' incentives hinged on how many of us cleared training. Since the online tests were in their hands, they made damn sure that the class passed. This led to a new situation, where we only paid attention to things that we knew would be important to the exams. The trainers realized that we were smart enough to cover their asses as well our own, and soon they too started slacking off. Grumpy Ganguly showed up periodically to conduct refresher voice and accent training classes. This meant practising more mock calls, where Surya would helpfully spice things up by adding technical questions to make the simulation that much more real.

My concerns at that point, however, were not promotions or sales targets or passing training or even earning enough incentives. I was drowning in worry over the the lunch date to beat all lunch dates.

6

ALL I WANT FOR CHRISTMAS

Our first month of technical training ended. While some people went home anxious about the online tests, some of us were already confident of making sales and making money. Stan, as usual, didn't give a rat's ass. Wribhu seemed to second Stan's opinion, and Dibya already knew that everything would be manipulated in order to get everyone to pass. I was the only person thinking not about the tests but about my lunch date.

On the cab home, Imsen smiled prettily at me and chatted about the weather, some movie she had watched and training stuff. All I was thinking about was kissing her. Before getting off the cab, she said, 'Hey, don't be late tomorrow I'll be cooking, but I need your help to go shopping, okay?' I nodded and smiled at her, tongue-tied as usual, but inside I was a positive torrent of emotions.

I reached home, showered and ate my food while watching some inane TV show which claimed to be about riding bikes and the open road but focused more on how lame Indian youngsters couldn't perform even the simplest tasks. However, even that epic comedy of hesitation and incompetence failed to change the channel that had lodged in my head: Channel Imsen, News at 10 with Imsen, CNN Imsen... I wondered what this meant. Then it hit me: Eureka! I had fallen for the woman with the beautiful voice and the glowing smile and the mango-shaped breasts.

The problem now was that if I told her, and she didn't feel the same way about me, then I might lose a friend. There might also be the situation where she liked me but the pesky fiancé back in the northeast commanded her loyalty. Pacing my room, I tried to figure out a way around the hypothetical roadblocks to my happiness.

One thing I knew for sure: I had to man up and tell her I liked her. Come what may, I had to tell her if I was to have even a chance at being with her. With these thoughts I went to bed, not noticing the noise from Ty's room or the fact that some girl on TV was pretty much baring her whole body.

On Christmas day, I woke up feeling like a million bucks. I must have been looking extra cheerful because Ty looked at me with his mouth open as if I had pulled a rabbit out of my rear. I guess I had been a sourpuss a bit longer than I should have. The only time you can say with impunity that you are over someone is when you start falling for other people. So I had fallen, and Ty was shocked and surprised. 'Merry Christmas, bro!' he yelled as he went off to work.

I called Imsen around ten. Hi, you awake?

'Yeah. When are you coming over?'

'In half an hour.'

'Great. See you soon.'

Did she mean 'Great, the useless lump has actually decided to plague me on my day off' or 'Great, we're going to have lunch together and an awesome Christmas'?

As you can see, I tend to get rather uncertain when I like someone. Maybe it was a case of diminished confidence in the aftermath of being cheated on. It's a very difficult rut to get out of, and the path to recovery is an arduous one. While most folks choose to get drunk, high and plastered in hopes of inducing enough cerebral damage to erase certain memories, some choose to eat too much and mope. The latter method is responsible for a lot of fat people peopling the streets. You eat too much because you are depressed and you are depressed because you eat too much. This is not a good method for getting over heartbreak. I call it 'The Circle of Fat'.

My patented method is a mix of everything. Mourning is only right, and any heartbreak should be suitably accompanied by tears, some minor depression and some overeating. But once you're ready to move out beyond the comfort of your four walls, you must indulge in life and make merry. Choose the intoxicant of your choice and put the pedal to the metal. These two stages will suffice in getting things back to normal and the heartbroken can get back into the game. You will notice at that point that your skills have become rusty from being in a serious relationship, but persistence is key. The final step to freedom from heartbreak and sappy memories is the moment you get laid again. This particular method was something I discovered post the Bidisha fiasco and midway through what I call in my head The Imsen Affair.

After a quick bath, I dragged my sorry ass to Imsen's flat. With beads of sweat trickling down my back, caused by a combination of nervousness and hypothetical performance anxiety, I rang her doorbell. She answered the door wearing the shortest shorts imaginable and a black tank top that made her top look just like her bottom—nicely rounded and large. She also looked very beautiful sans make-up.

As she pottered in the kitchen, making a list of supplies to buy, I gently descended into a cesspool of terrors fuelled by my potential inadequacies. Did I look good enough? Did my breath smell? Was my underwear clean? Was my deodorant working? These vital questions were sapping my will to seduce her. So I did what any guy should do when faced with a hot girl with whom he has prospects and is being hamstringed by his own paranoia. I went straight to her bathroom and polished the doorknob, spanked the dolphin, choked the chicken, effectively defusing the rocket in my pocket. This might seem like an extreme step, but it certainly calmed me down. I was now ready to be charming, funny, and courteously sexy. In short, I was going to act like a Bollywood hero.

When I emerged from the bathroom, Imsen had changed

into tracks and was waiting for me with a grocery bag. 'Let's go, handsome. Time for some veggie shopping.'

'After you, beautiful. And let's get some meat while we are at it,' I replied with a wink, and almost immediately kicked myself. Let's get some meat. What a sucky line! Obviously, the chicken needed to have been choked harder. However, Imsen did laugh at that. And, well, if a girl likes you, she will laugh at your fart jokes too—so I guess I wasn't doing too badly.

For those of you who have never gone grocery shopping in Kolkata, please do so. It's an adventure for the sense of smell at par with a visit to a public toilet. Maybe I'm exaggerating a little, but the damn place did stink. It put quite a dampener on the conversation I was having with Imsen. It wasn't like we were solving world hunger or putting the final touches on the plans for world peace, but the conversation was going pretty nicely—till we entered the market. From then on, the stink of fish, chicken shit, dead meat and the weird-smelling pesticide that they put in veggies totally killed the mood. I kept my mouth shut until we'd made our way out of the bazaar. In fact, the assault on my senses had neutered me temporarily.

Imsen went for a bath once we got back to her flat. After the shopping expedition, I needed one too—I smelt like a ripe buffalo.

Imsen cooked the chicken and it was delicious. We ate and, in the delightful lull of a full stomach, I had a smoke. We talked about friends, family, work at the call centre and the kind of movies we liked. We hung out until it got pretty late in the day. The sun had ended its journey and night had taken over while we talked. We had quite a bit in common and, while we learnt more about each other, I kind of forgot to be on guard. Most guys who are out to seduce a girl, or even woo her, will try and put on a different persona from the one they actually have. The first five dates or meetings will always have the guy showing his best side in order to have a decent chance of snagging the girl. However, I was enjoying the conversation and loving her company to the extent that I totally forgot to pretend.

Incredibly enough, revealing your true personality does wonders for your love life—that's what I discovered that day. (Although, if your true persona is that of a douchebag, please keep projecting the nice-guy façade.)

Imsen had pulled out a pile of books for me to borrow from. As I leant over her to grab a title I wanted to read, I also turned to ask her something. This particular move brought me within kissing distance quite unintentionally. Her face was so close to mine that I could smell her hair. Time seemed to slow down and I found myself moving closer to her face until our lips met. It was sweet and innocent, a bit of a soul kiss, actually. Imsen kissed me back with a look on her face that told me she wanted this as well. I sat back and smiled sheepishly, wondering how that had happened. Then I pulled her close and kissed her again. I think we must have spent close to ten minutes just kissing and holding each other while the doorbell kept ringing.

Imsen finally pulled away to answer the door. While she spoke to her neighbour, I waited in her room, with a pounding heart and a goofy smile on my face. I was thinking of how sweet her lips tasted and also about how her fiancé would probably castrate me. But the fact that she had kissed me back drowned all other thought and made me want to turn cartwheels.

When Imsen came back to the room, I held her close again and kissed her deeply. She sighed. Then she held my hand and led me to the bed. As I lay on top of her, I had this feeling, where you know what is about to follow and yet your imagination cannot quite match what comes next. She pulled my clothes off and hers as well and... Ahem, we made love. Her skin was incredibly soft and she was very open in bed. Some women can be quite dull in bed. No oral, no doggie, nothing but missionary. Imsen, happily for me, was quite daring.

Afterwards, as I lay utterly exhausted in a pool of sweat, Imsen played with my hair and kissed me sweetly. I realized then that no words of adoration or endless love had passed between us. There was no post-coital awkwardness. As I grinned to myself, Imsen pulled me on top of her and we got right back to it.

It was a Very Merry Christmas indeed.

7

CLEARING TECHNICAL TRAINING

Come Monday morning, I felt like everything was right with the world. I guess great sex can do that to a person.

When Imsen called me, we spoke like everything was just the same. She talked as if nothing had happened, and I wondered what was wrong. Not that she sounded disturbed or anything—but if you have sex with someone, you expect them to be a bit warmer. She sounded a little too cold for someone who had been in bed with me only a few hours ago. Anyway, I decided to think nothing of it and proceeded to eat a big breakfast of eggs, ham and bacon in preparation for sleeping all day long. The big breakfast was just a small part of the things I had to do to keep my body going while working nights.

The adjustments we had to make because of the night shifts were endless—from the timings of meals, to the timings of bowel movements (which usually happened at work), everything was topsy-turvy. The greatest victims of the night shift in no particular order are bodily and mental health, social life and general chances at moving into a better job. When you sleep all day and work all night, the world just passes you by.

The cab that Monday night came late as usual. By now we had gotten so used to their incompetence that we had stopped complaining. In return for the transport department's general lack of logic in route planning and punctuality, we smoked in the cabs. Apparently, Wribhu, Stan and Dibya had started smoking stuff more powerful than tobacco in the cabs—the drivers on their routes had started complaining.

Stan smoked up because he was Stan. Wribhu did it to be cool. But why did Dibya do it? He was older than us, he had worked before and he supported a family. A drug habit was the last thing he needed, and so I told him that to his face. To this, he said, 'When you have been doing night shifts as long as I have, you need something extra to keep you going. Sometimes, it's money and promotions; and, sometimes, being stoned helps when there is no money and no promotion.'

I accepted this explanation, silently hoping that my friends would not get caught. I guess I sound preachy for someone who also got stoned just as regularly, but I never did so at work. Smoking up and being high at work, in my opinion, was stupid and the sort of thing that could get you fired. But Dibya was right in a way: we could not get promoted till we had been in the organization for at least eighteen months. That's a year and a half, a long time for someone to wait for their IJP. The whole system rested on nepotism and 'favours'—and not all of us had Internal Jaan Pehchaan. So what could one do, except to smoke some weed to take the edge off one's frustration?

What I did not know at that point, however, was that a lot of people smoked up at work—from the managers and higher-ups to the security guards and the canteen-wallahs. So, while you were getting high, you could actually do some sideways Jaan Pehchaan.

In the meantime, we were fast approaching the end of our technical training period and Surya was grilling us daily. In addition to passing online technical exams, we had to pass a final mock call, where not only would we have to solve a technical problem for a pretend customer but also clear a quality sheet. The quality sheet, for those who don't know, was a list of dos and don'ts during the call, which was supposed to help evaluate your commitment to making every call a good call and a 'wow' experience. The mock call and the quality sheet together were making life hell for all of us in general, and Imsen's coldness was driving me nuts in particular.

One night, when Imsen finally got up to take a bathroom break, I followed suit, not caring what crap was being taught. I waited outside the ladies' restroom. When she came out, she smiled. In that instant, I knew that I was simply being paranoid about the whole coldness thing. She came up close to me and said, 'Kris, did you know that fraternization among colleagues is not encouraged at Big Blue?'

'Um, no, I had no idea,' I said. Her behaviour immediately made sense. Imsen was saving both our asses.

In a hushed whisper, she added: 'But that won't stop me from doing the hokey-pokey with you when we get home.'

I must have worn the biggest, stupidest grin in the world that night.

When we got back to the training room, Surya started to explain for the hundredth time the stack parameters which would fetch us our incentives once we hit the floor. Once he was done with his lecture, he turned his attention to the class. Most days, Stan would be grilled and drilled like crazy by Surya. From mistakes on the quality sheet to mistakes on technical knowledge, Stan was doing everything wrong. At first, we all thought that Stan was a little on the slow side. Later, we realized that he made all the mistakes possible just to piss off Surya. Once Surya got frustrated enough, he usually focused his energies on everyone else in the class and grilled everyone harder than ever. Mock call after mock call would ensue and, in his corner, Stan would silently laugh about making everyone's life miserable. That boy really had the devil in him.

Typically, a fresher like me took the mock calls very seriously because once we hit the production floor there would be very little time for learning. Dibya had worked in a technical process before, so he knew all the tricks of the trade and was coping quite well. Stan simply did not give a rat's ass; he wanted to get paid—everything else was just nonsense to him. This was something a lot of people did. They joined training, pick up their salaries and then quit. Since there was no real work for at least the first three months, they simply sat back and relaxed, raking in the money. Some were even smart enough to keep failing training so that they would get moved to the next batch and keep getting trained. They could stretch this to at least three training sessions for a grand total of a year of training. Once they were forced to hit the production floor, they quit and moved on to the next company. Stan might not have had exactly this in mind, but a few of the people in our training class did. Like Uncle Biswajeet, who had been in training since two batches before us.

The dude was about thirty-eight years old, had worked at call centres when they first started in India and had never been promoted. He had worked for more than five years in one place, and then spent a year here, a year there, enjoying training and the high salary he commanded because of his years of experience. Uncle Biswajeet was notoriously lazy, slept in class to different renditions of snores and was Surya's worst nightmare. He knew nothing, learnt nothing and wanted to learn nothing. Surya tried his best to train Biswajeet enough to pass, but, as the saying goes, a one-legged man cannot win an ass-kicking competition.

If the mock calls were a hated part of technical training, the floor walks were the icing on the cake. The entire training team was led to the production floor, which was on the fourteenth floor of the same building, and we got to spend time with agents taking real calls. We got to buddy up with them and, using a phone jack, heard live technical calls. However, the most exciting part was hearing how easy the customers were to sell to and how easy their problems were—at least, most of the time. One agent I jacked up with told me that Americans hated the Indian accent and in the early days of the call centre would abuse Indians agents like crazy, but with time they had gotten used to us. He also told me how big the sales incentives could get: some agents on the floor made more than fifty grand every month. This was the one call centre where agents were making as much as the management—and we were eager to get our share of the incentive pie.

Most of us got tired of the jacking in and listening to calls routine quite early and turned to the other fun part of a floor walk: checking out all the girls on the floor. Imsen would also get looks from the guys on the floor, which made me feel a little jealous.

Though the floor walks were fun, there were very few of them. On these select occasions, we were left to our own devices for at least three hours. Usually, Stan, Dibya, and Wribhu disappeared for a bit and then came back stoned.

During the last two weeks of technical training, everywhere I looked, fellow trainees were trying to find out from agents who'd passed the training what could be asked in the mock calls. This frantic activity was also fuelled by the revelation that our process was a 500 seater, which meant that only 500 agents were required out of

Kolkata. We were the last batch and would make up the last fifteen of that particular 500. Whoever had enjoyed the fruits of extended training now had to pass the mock calls as there was no next batch of trainees they could be grouped with. Uncle Biswajeet looked like he would have a stroke from the strain. The normally sleepy Biswajeet was now a tornado of activity and learning and Surya looked incredibly relieved that he was finally getting serious.

Everyone else was trying feverishly to memorize solutions to all the technical problems that could arise. They tried to learn up all the symptoms that a computer could show and tried to double-guess the various tricks the assessor could use to throw them off the scent. They even tried to memorize the commands and various steps necessary to solve certain technical problems. I found all this useless because if the assessor wanted to fail you he would. Besides, we had access to Google during the mock call. If one could identify the symptoms, one could find the solution too.

Indrajit's favourite part was asking us: 'Okay, now the customer's hard disk is not working. What do you sell him?' People in the class would answer: 'Sell him a new hard disk.' To this he would yell: 'NO! You tell him that his hard disk is old and that is why it is not working. Thus his computer is also old and will soon stop working entirely, and the customer should buy a new laptop. Buying a new computer will cost almost as much as buying a new hard disk and installing it. So, for the same price, the customer can get a whole new computer. If he refuses, sell him a new hard disk, and sell him an external hard disk in case his hard disk crashes again like the old one. Explain to him how this will help save his data, and also try to sell him a hardware warranty, explaining how it is cheaper than buying spare parts.'

To Indrajit, every problem was an opportunity to sell something, and God help the hapless soul who did not pitch a sale in his or her mock call. Surya leant the same way and believed that a good technician could be a good salesman because, you see, when you solve someone's problem with a computer all the way in America while sitting at your workstation in India, the American will believe that you are pretty good at what you do and trust you and your recommendations. Whichever way you took it, the end goal was to sell something.

As if managing the mock call and the technical training wasn't bad enough, next they threw their user tool into the mix. It all became a bit of a circus. We used a tool that was connected to a database that would help us identify the customer, find out the previous problems they had faced, see what products still remained to be sold to them and find out how many days they had left on their warranty. Navigating the tool was a whole new ball game. There were at least three ways to identify the customer: through name, telephone number or email. This was not much of a problem, but logging the case required real-time documentation, just in case things went belly-up on a call if the tool crashed—which, it appeared, it did quite a bit.

There were instances when a customer asked for a refund because a certain problem had not been solved or he had been misled into buying things. The formats for case-logging were a part of the mock call, and we prayed that we would remember the whole damn thing. Case notes and the case-logging had saved many an agent from being fired or blamed for a refund. The refund itself was expected, but there was a particular type of refund we dreaded: the chargeback.

In this case, the customer would not call us for a refund but instead contact his bank and get their money refunded directly. When a chargeback is initiated, the bank runs a cross-check. And when too many chargebacks occur against a company, then they block the credit card services or the payment gateway. Big Blue had been barred by Amex and Mastercard after five chargebacks, so they were keen on not getting barred by others. Thus, when a chargeback occurred, the last cases were examined, the calls were scrutinized and someone had to take the blame. Hence the importance of cases notes depicting what was done on a call. If the agent had followed all the steps and left no room for finger-pointing, then he (or she) would get off with a warning. If any fault was found, instant termination happened.

Most days, Imsen would sit next to me to practise mock calls. Being near her made the night shifts bearable and the lousy canteen food acceptable. The horrid training period began to feel like one of the best times in my life. However, there was a slight glitch in my happy story: I was not sure exactly what I felt about Imsen.

When she spoke to her fiancé, who called during every lunch break, there were no pangs of jealousy. I felt none of the emotions that should apply in a situation where one is in love. There was chemistry, friendship and lust, but love was simply not on the scene. This did not, however, prevent me from sleeping with her. On the contrary, I think it made it more fun. No commitments and no strings attached worked for us both. She never told me she loved me and I never said the words either. We shared a silent understanding that we were only friends with benefits.

Finally, the mock calls arrived. I knew how to identify the problems and the logical steps to take, so I was well-prepared. When I was chosen by Surya as the first trainee to take a call, I was the very picture of coolness. Strangely enough, Indrajit and Surya were going to take our mock calls, while all along they had led us to believe that someone else would come to assess us. I sat down in front of one of the many computers in the training room and waited for the mock call to begin. I prepared the user tool and got my copy of the quality sheet open to remind me not to miss any important points.

'Tring, tring!' said Indrajit, indicating that there was a call waiting.

I opened with the mandatory call script greeting: 'Thank you for calling Big Blue Technical Services. May I have your first and last names please?'

Instead of stating his name, Indrajit began a litany of abuses and complaints. 'You guys are a bunch of thieves and scoundrels! I want my money back, and no excuses. You guys sold me a lemon of a computer.' His words, of course, were peppered with the choicest abuses. Asshole, bastard, dirty Indian beggar, monkey people, hairy Hindu, etc.

I was a little taken aback. But, knowing Indrajit, this was just a way to fluster me. I gathered my wits and calmly said, 'Sir, I will be more than pleased to help you out with your problem, but in order to do so I need some information to identify your account. I apologize on behalf of Big Blue and will help you to the best of my ability. May I please have your first and last names?'

After this, Indrajit stated how he had called to get a virus removed and was sold an antivirus that did not work, and he thought that the virus was still in the computer. I offered to clean the computer of the virus and then promised a refund if he was not satisfied with the services.

After this little drama was through, Surya asked me the steps to cleaning up a virus manually. I told him the steps to take a remote session on the customer's computer, stated the disclaimers and proceeded with a registry clean-up followed by a scan by our tools. The tools package to speed up the customer's computer was touted as an exclusive feature and a key selling point, even though it was a freebie from Big Blue. After that I got the customer (Indrajit, that is) to acknowledge that his problems were fixed and pitched for a sale which was refused. I closed the call after telling him we would send a survey form via email for this particular technical session.

Indrajit came over and checked my case documentation on the user tool. He looked happy with what he saw and said, 'You're a very sharp boy. Remember, never lose your temper at the customer. If you get angry, then channel that anger to sell. Good job.'

I was pleased as punch. Now that my mock call was over, I had the whole night to do nothing or anything I wanted. Our shift timings had changed to 1.30 a.m., which meant that we would get off training at eleven in the daytime. Once you stay awake for nights for about two months in a row, no opportunity is to be missed. I quickly headed over to a plump sofa in the reception area and gave myself up to sleep.

By the time I woke up the shift for the day was over and Imsen was gently patting my head so that we could leave. The results would be announced at the next shift because apparently some people had failed the mock calls and would be doing them all over again. This was called retraining and spanned a five-day period, at the end of which the mock calls would take place again. However, due to chor-porate diligence, there would be no real training— the failing trainees would be told to practice on their own and their mock calls would be exactly the same as before. God help those who failed retraining.

Imsen and I boarded our cab. She pinched me and whispered, 'Better catch up on your sleep after you get home, handsome. It's time for your retraining. At my place.' Now, if that did not wake a guy up, what would?

After spending a few hours at her place, I made my way home weary but satisfied. Everything seemed to be working out: I had a girl but no girlfriend; sex but no responsibilities. The future was ahead of me, and it looked bright.

That night at work, we found out that those who had cleared the technical training mock calls would be forming a transition team led by Surya. We would be rookies on the production floor for a month and then distributed among the existing teams. Our initial log-in would be for three hours for the first week, then six hours for the second week and third weeks, and then a full shift for the last week. It was important to do well because that would decide which teams we would get into. Some teams had horrid team leaders who would pile on the pressure to make sales and chew you out for each and every little thing. These teams also had sucky graveyard shifts most of the time. The good teams had great team leaders who would pitch in if a call was not going well. They also got the opening shifts, where the working hours were somewhat normal—relatively speaking, of course.

In transition, the sales we made would also fetch us sales incentives. We were taken to a training room near the production floor and made to wait by Surya. He came back with two guys who looked incredibly similar. We all thought they must be brothers, or at least related, but it turned out that they weren't. These two were our SMEs, or subject matter experts. They were our support system on the floor and would look after us and keep us from, as Surya put it, 'fucking up'. On closer inspection, I saw that one SME had a slight squint and the other one was shorter than him. The squinty one's name was Lav and the short one was Kushal—everyone called them Lav and Kush. We were also introduced to Neel, who would be our quality analyst. It was his job to screen and scrub our calls and give us points on the quality parameter.

The three of them then launched into a whole set of PowerPoint presentations and lectures on how to get our data 'green'. Since they did the whole presentation with the lights off, I promptly fell asleep, using Imsen as my cover. By the time I woke up, Lav and Kush were splitting us into two teams for easy handling. Imsen, Dibya and Wribhu went into Lav's team, and I went to Kush with Stan. I did not know it then, but we were about to become pawns in a rivalry that everyone else in the company was privy to.

8

HITTING THE FLOOR

As luck would have it, all the transition teams had to do the graveyard shift so that the teams on the floor could be moved to an earlier timing. This gave the older teams a bit of a rest and got the transition team prepared for the herculean task of taking calls. This would now be our third month on the graveyard shift.

I had taken to smoking a pack a day, beginning from when I boarded the cab and ending when only when I reached home to eat and sleep. The first smoke was to wake me up and the rest would help me stay awake. Between the graveyard shift, lots of coffee and the cigarettes, I felt like a zombie and a vampire all rolled into one. I hardly got to see the sun and had lost quite a bit of weight. I hoped to get a long leave once the transition month was over so that I could go home to the hills and sleep. My mind and body perpetually craved sleep. Every weekly off-day, I slept for at least fourteen hours. And still I felt sleepy. Once I was on call, however, I would light up like a Diwali cracker.

I called this the Smell of Money effect. Each call was an opportunity to sell, a chance to make more incentives and more cash. The technical aspects were just a cover to help make the sale.

Before we took calls for the first week, Kush called us into a training room close to the production floor for a team 'hurdle'—apparently, Kush thought that a team meeting involved an obstacle race, not a group huddle. He was full of vim and vigour and said, 'Any problems you have, I will handle. You take your calls and make sales. If you cannot fix a problem, call me—I will fix it. If you do not know a procedure on the user tool, call me—I will do it. All I ask is that you make sales. I have your IDs for the user tools and will give them to you. This is serious business now. Your honeymoon period is over. Let's make some sales and get some numbers.'

For a transition team, making sales was not an important parameter. But the way Kush went on about selling had us thinking otherwise. He informed us that our data was being counted from the transition period onwards and thus to maintain a good record we had to make sales. Though this sounded rather fishy, we went with it.

We swiped our ID cards and were ushered to a set of workstations, with Lav's team taking up workstations on the opposite bay. Lav and Kush eyed each other like two angry bulls looking to mate with the same cow. They were just a little spittle away from frothing at the mouth.

Imsen waved at me and smiled, I waved back. Dibya

and Wribhu looked grim and sat at their workstations with grumpy faces. Stan sat next to me, leant over and said, 'These two monkeys, Lav and Kush, hate each other. They have been on the floor since day one of the process and both are up for promotion for the same post in the next IJP.' After passing on this little titbit, Stan sat back in his chair, started opening his user tools and began preparing to log in.

Kush walked up to everyone's system and whispered hushed instructions. 'Check the user tool and find out what they don't have.' 'Keep building rapport and dropping hints that they need to buy something to fix their issue.' 'Don't pitch outright, soften the customer up and transfer the call over to me.'

Finally, when we did log in, we put on our headsets and waited for the user tool to light up, indicating that we had a call. For three hours, we sat looking at our systems—none of us got any calls. Lav and Kush started checking the queue to figure out where we stood on the agent waiting list. Somehow, neither team was showing up on the queue. It turned out that we had not yet been entered into the system by the senior techs in Gurgaon. And so our first day on calls turned out to be a total flop.

I took a smoke break with Imsen and sauntered outside, where Stan and the boys were waiting. In between puffs of a cigarette, Dibya and Wribhu described how stunned Uncle Biswajeet had been on finding out he had cleared the technical training. The conversation eventually turned to Lav and Kush's rivalry. Apparently, every transition batch was their battlefield and they competed with each other on sales figures. We had entered a warzone and been put on opposite sides. While Wribhu and Stan seemed to take it in their stride, Dibya warned us that this could very well affect our careers at Big Blue. Stan laughed at this because he wasn't intending on sticking around long enough to build anything.

Kush had a strategy chalked out for us. It revolved around solving the issue, chatting up the customer and convincing the customer that his problem would be solved by buying something. If it was a software glitch, we had to sell them a warranty. If that option was there already, we had to sell an extension on the plan they had with us. Fascinating ruses and ploys were discussed and Kush went through a range of white lies we could tell.

I looked at Imsen closely. In the last three months, she had gotten much thinner. She had been curvy to begin with, but she was now approaching size zero and beyond. Stan looked malnourished, like a bodybuilder from Ethopia. I looked at myself in the plate-glass mirror and noticed that my face had gotten leaner and had a hard look to it. We were all losing weight because of all the weird lifestyle we were leading.

Another thing I noticed about call centre workers, myself included, was how little we conversed with the outside world. I mean, I spoke to people, but rarely ever did I have a conversation with people who I did not work with.

This was my world—where I worked at night and talked to Americans halfway across the world, selling in dollars and getting paid in rupees. I rarely even saw Ty because he had almost the same timings as me and we mostly communicated via texts. The last conversation I'd had with my mother must have lasted five minutes at the most. Usually, I was either too sleepy to talk or I was at work and my phone was sitting in my locker. I was, however, secretly glad—most of my conversations with my mother seemed to revolve around how well my peers were doing and how I was wasting my life.

'You know that boy James you went to school with?' she would say.

'Yes, Mum.'

'He is now a commercial pilot. He makes lakhs a month. He takes his parents on holidays abroad every year.'

Silence at my end.

'You know your cousin Bharat? He is an engineer in Dubai. He just bought a BMW and got his mother a diamond set.'

Silence.

'When will you do something with your life, son? All this working at night like a night watchman is taking you nowhere. How long will this industry last? How secure is your future? Do you get any medical insurance or pension? When will you be secure enough to get married? We are not getting any younger...'

This was generally the point where I told my mother that

I needed to sleep and hung up on her. She usually called back to ask when I would drag my sorry ass home. After a few rounds of this, I started to keep my phone on silent. My mind had bigger things on it then stress over where my life was going. I needed sales, and in a bad way...

The second day on calls went well, but not as well as it should have. My customer was a Gloria Weinstein from New York and her computer was shutting down within a few minutes of booting. She knew very little about how computers actually worked, and that was where the real problem lay.

'So, Gloria, do you have to restart the computer after the screen goes black?'

'No. If I move the mouse the screen comes back on.'

What was happening here was that her power settings on the computer were configured to turn off the screen after a certain period of time.

I chatted with Gloria and asked her how life was in New York. She spoke about how it was the greatest city in the world and other things I had no interest in hearing but had pretend to want to know. This sort of fakery was more tiring than the shifts we were doing. I took a remote of her computer, fixed the setting and pitched for a sale. She turned me down and Kush, who was standing behind me, listening to the call, looked like he would have a fit right there. Once the call was done, he told me to switch my status on the user tool to a break and called me over to his system.

'Kris, what the fuck were you doing?'

'I solved her issue and pitched for a sale.'

'Did you check what the options were on the customer?'

'Um, no.'

'What was the issue?'

'It was a simple power configuration setting.'

'Kris, when you do something simple for the customer, you have to make it look complicated! Do a disk clean-up, clear the prefetch and temp folders. If need be, run a virus scan. If you do not create the need or the urgency, if you do not make the customer feel that they have to buy something that will help them, you will get no sale. I have heard your English—it is very good. Use it and sell, okay?'

'Got it, Kush.'

'When you have a customer next, let me make the pitch and you listen and learn.'

Before he could think of more bullshit to spout at me, Uncle Biswajeet started gesturing frantically. At first glance, I thought he was having a heart attack on the floor. Turned out that he had a customer who had bought two new computers and wanted to buy warranties for both of them. The normally slow-as-a-sloth Kush suddenly leapt into action. He instructed Uncle Biswajeet to tell the customer to speak with his technical supervisor who would help him make the transaction. Once Uncle Biswajeet handed the call to him, Kush was all butter and cream. He switched the call to the loudspeaker so that we could all hear his pitch.

'Hello, David, my name is Kush and I am the floor

technical supervisor. What I understand is that you want to purchase warranties for your two new computers?'

'That's right.'

'So will you be getting the full premium plan for three years?'

'Um, how much is that?'

'Well, sir, since you are a valued customer… The price is normally $399, but I can get you a discount.'

'Wow, that's expensive!'

'David, there is a sizeable discount,' Kush interjected. 'Let me enter my supervisor's code and see what we have for you.'

'Okay.'

The catch here was that there was no special discount or a supervisor's code; as a matter of fact, there was not even a premium plan—just a one-year or two-year or three-year plan. The discount was a discount that all customers who bought the full plan would get.

'So, David, I see here that the full plan for both computers will cost you only $599, at $299 each. You are getting a discount of $200 and premium support for three years.'

Here, David started hesitating because, hey, $599 is a shitload of money, even if you are American. Kush had shown the customer the $200 discount carrot; now he started showing the customer the stick.

'The thing is, David, that this discount is for a limited period only. It will expire today. On any other day, it will cost you the full price, which is $799.'

'Um, maybe I should check with another company,' said David.

'Sir, we are the cheapest and yet the best in the market. But you know that already. Let's do it, sir, its savings and value for money.'

The customer, if he is rich and in a hurry, would readily hand over his credit card details—and that is exactly what happened.

Kush entered the details, ran the transactions and, after handing the customer back to Uncle Biswajeet, gloated: 'And that, team, is how we make a sale.'

In my head I thought: 'And that, team, is what we call fraud.' But, hey, who was I to argue with an SME? Kush then turned towards Lav's bay and loudly announced: 'PEOPLE, WE HAVE A SALE OF $599 BY BISWAJEET!'

This was followed by lots of clapping and cheering. Uncle Biswajeet looked bewildered, Kush wore the kind of smile that a Hindi movie villain has whilst raping the hero's sister and across the bay Lav was grinding his teeth.

'Come on, you useless fools, make a sale or I will screw your happiness!' screamed Lav.

Suddenly, it was war.

Every sale was announced with gusto, every announcement was a barrage at the other team. We were trying to sell everything we could and pitching every product possible. It was exciting and tiring, but I was yet to make a sale. Imsen was ploughing through her customers and selling on almost every call, Dibya was using his experience to milk his customers for all they were worth. While they were taking the whole thing very seriously, Stan was busy taking the customer's trip. He was making life difficult for the customer and enjoying it. Apparently, some customer had called in drunk and refused to follow Stan's instructions, so Stan had him switch his computer on and off for about fifteen times. This was the sort of mischief he got up to. It was like when a monkey gets hold of a laser gun—fun to watch, but painful for all concerned.

I, on the other hand, was trying my best and getting flubbed at every turn. Kush came up to me and said, 'We need to talk.' I knew he was going to chew me out for not selling, but there was nothing I could do. I felt like a convict on death row taking his last steps.

In an environment where the competition is not only trying to overtake you but also bury you, there is no room for non-performance. In a call centre, the bottom line is always business and sales, no matter what kind of process you may be in. I was guilty of committing the cardinal sin of no sales in a sales-driven technical process. In simple terms, I was not doing what I had been hired for. These were the little insights that Kush revealed to me once I'd walked over to his workstation.

Over the three remaining weeks of transition, almost everyone made sales. Even Stan made a sale, much against his will. He had had the good fortune of getting a customer who wanted to buy warranty and an antivirus program. We sold antiviruses too and activated them and downloaded them over the Internet. I was still sitting on zero sales, with just five days to clear transition. Even the crazy-monkey sex with Imsen was not doing much for my mood. I felt useless, like a fifth wheel on a car or a third leg on a runner.

My average handling time was below forty-five minutes for customers, my surveys were always positive and my resolution rate was 100 per cent. Even my quality scores were good. But Kush kept pointing out that this meant nothing since it would not get me into a good team, nor was I making any incentives out of this. He had almost given up with me.

But then one call changed it all.

'Thank you for calling Big Blue. My name is Kris. How may I help you today?'

'Hi, my name is Karen and I want my computer fixed. It's not powering on.'

I then proceeded to perform a power-drain, which is a procedure to drain static electricity from computers. In the meantime, I explained how if the computer did not power on it was a hardware issue and she would need to take the computer to a local tech. But if it did power on, then a software glitch might be causing the problem.

The computer powered on.

After this, Kush took over and got Karen to subscribe with us—and I got my first sale. As it happened, Karen had four other computers and was a rich old lady. She bought three-year warranties for the other computers also, as well as hardware warranties. Suddenly, I had the highest sales amount on the entire production floor!

As Kush announced that I had made close to a $2,000 sale on just one call, the entire floor stood up to take a look at me. It was an ill-deserved honour because it was Kush who had done all the pitching, but none of the other teams knew that. Lav came over and shook my hand, despite my feeble protests that this was all Kush's doing.

Kush had told the old lady that she had a virus infecting her system. This was not true, but he made it seem so by downloading a free spyware tool. He passed the spyware off for viruses and told her that her other computers were also infected. After making a show of cleaning the virus, he sold her warranties for her computer, her husband's computer and the other computers in the house. But the icing on the cake was when he told her that this now qualified her as a customer who could buy cut-rate warranties on the hardware as well.

She bought it all, and I felt like a con artist.

I was instantly famous on the floor. I was the guy who had sold more on one call than most people in a month. Kush had set expectations—and I had to meet them.

In other words, I was fucked.

9

I AM NOT YOUR SALES MESSIAH

In the last two days of transition, people from our team of fifteen were picked by the team leaders. While most went to decent teams, Uncle Biswajeet and Stan were put in Manjeet Kaur's team. Manjeet was an abusive hard-ass, famous for making people extend their shifts if they did not meet their sales targets. Dibya went to the team headed by Rina Talukdar, a team-leader-cum-assistant-manager and a pretty fine-looking woman who was rumoured to have gotten her promotions after doing some after-hours entertainment for the managers. Wribhu went into the same team. Imsen and I joined Chiranjib Majumder, who was the nicest team-leader-cum-assistant-manager on the floor. He also was the most experienced of all the team leaders, which meant that he had been in the same position for the last five years.

Imsen and I were drafted into Chiranjib's team for our exceptional sales figures—he was hoping that we would be able to boost the sales figures for his team, which had been lagging behind for quite a while. He had big hopes of the two of us, but me more than Imsen for my one-call sales record. I could have cheerfully strangled Kush for this little favour of his.

I wanted to explain the facts to Chiranjib, but he was too busy with something or the other and I ended up face-to-face with my SME Piyush instead. Piyush was the kind of person who could not take no for an answer. He was also the kind of boot-licker who got promotions by the sheer force of ass-kissing. It was way beyond his abilities to solve any technical issues or even to substitute for any agent. My attempts to explain how my sales abilities were over-hyped were met with a blank stare. The only thing Piyush was good at, I heard, was seducing the ladies—he had apparently slept with almost every pretty thing on the floor.

Out team had twelve people in it; not counting Imsen and me, they had the same zombie expressions you'll find on anyone who has worked at a call centre for too long. They ignored the two of us as if we carried the Ebola virus. No one spoke to us or acknowledged us. Not that we gave a rat's ass about that. Imsen sat next to me. While I tried desperately to make a sale, she seemed to find it no effort at all. I tried everything to sell and utilized all the points that Indrajit had outlined. I created a need for the product in the mind of the customer, I tried to highlight the massive discounts on offer, but I still could not sell to save my life.

In the meantime, Chiranjib was bearing down on me. I

had spent almost a week in his team and was not yet selling. Imsen was literally pulling my weight, and while she was gradually accepted by the team, I was looked upon as the pariah who had no use. Chiranjib called me and asked me why I was not selling, even though I had the capability to do so according to Kush and Piyush. I told him I that was doing everything possible. He eventually came to the conclusion that with me it was not an issue of skill but an issue of will. I simply did not want to sell.

Things came to a head-on collision when Indrajit was called in to try and motivate me. He was strangely sympathetic, unlike in class, and seemed genuinely concerned with trying to find out what my problem was.

'What is the excuse customers make when they refuse to buy something?' he asked.

'Um, they usually say they have no money. Or that they will think about it.'

'Hmm. What do you do to make it appear to the customer that they must buy the warranty? Do you enforce the suggestion that the product they are buying is absolutely essential?'

'Yes. I try, but…'

Indrajit cut me off. 'That's where the problem is. You must create the need, hype the product and make the need appear immediate. That's how you'll sell.'

While I tried to understand how to make a three-year warranty appear to be more than it was, Imsen walked over to me. She asked if I was hungry. In the canteen, between mouthfuls of rice and pork cooked with bamboo shoots, she pointed out the real reason why I was not able to sell.

'Kris, you are too honest to sell anything. When you have to sell a warranty, you must tell a white lie to make the customer believe that the three-year plan is better and different from the other plans. You can call it premium services or highlight the manual virus removal aspect or anything you want. Be creative, and you will make the sale.'

'But, Imsen, isn't that cheating the customer?'

'Look, Kris, when they buy something they buy a good product. So what if we sell with a lie? At least we do more than any technical service they will ever get. Cheer up! Get busy selling. Who knows, if you meet your target, I might just do something special for you.'

Now cash incentives and goodies are fine, but when someone offers you sales incentives of the bedroom variety you really jump at it. I was determined to sell something not just to save face and my spot on the team but also for what Imsen had promised me. My will to sell was now at its peak.

In the meantime, Chiranjib had put Piyush on my case and told him to give me all the support I needed. I soon realized that though Piyush was willing he was not really able. The guy knew very little about any technical issue and if anyone asked him for help on a particular task he simply pointed them towards the resident expert on the topic. He was equally inept at sales and pitching. I put him on call with a customer who was unable to decide whether to buy one external hard disk or two. Piyush kept insisting that the customer needed 'two hard dix, sir, you need two hard dix'. Suffice it to say, I never asked him for any help after that.

I gave it my best. I tried so hard that I near about lost my voice pitching to every customer who landed on my console. I double-checked the user tool every time to make sure that I knew exactly what the customers did not have. If they had a full three-year warranty, I pitched the hardware warranty; if they had that, I pitched the antivirus. But if they had everything already, then I tried to sell them extra hardware—which meant convincing them of the fine uses and applications of an operating system DVD or an external disk drive. Yet, despite all my attempts, I kept falling flat on my face.

In the last week of the month, I decided that it was time to take off the kid gloves and do the unthinkable—I would pitch to sell with a white lie to sell. However, all it took was one elderly customer to make me realize that I was too soft-hearted to sell anything.

After running a virus scan with our patented virus detector, Badware Bytes, which actually picked up spyware that almost everyone had, I was about ready to pass off the spyware as a virus.

'Kris, what are those things that the Badware program is picking up?' the lady on the phone asked.

'Ma'am, those are viruses that have infected your system.'

'Oh my! How did I get so many?'

'Well, you can get them from email or free games or free software from the Internet.'

'What can I do now, Kris? Can you help me?'

I told her that I could, that I would remove the viruses, but she needed stronger protection. In fact, she needed an antivirus much like the McCurseSpree that we currently had a discount on.

'How much will it cost me after the discount?'

'Ma'am, its $79 for three years of McCurseSpree after the discount, with the added bonus that any viruses that infect your computer after installation will be dealt with manually by us.'

The last statement was true insofar that we did take care of viruses manually, but we did so even if the customer did not purchase the antivirus.

'It's a little expensive, but I guess I do need it. After my husband died last month, money has been a little tight, but I will make ends meet somehow. Okay, how do I get it? How do I install it?'

It was then that I realized that I was not cut out for selling. I sold her the antivirus and installed it, but I felt like a crook all the while. I took her money, earned a pat on the back from Chiranjib and a wink from Imsen. But I felt like shit. No one else at Big Blue seemed to have this problem. Or maybe they did, but they had long since resigned themselves to the fact that if they did not sell someone else would. Maybe my conscience too would die a steady and slow death under the burden of sales targets and meeting expectations. However, for that moment, it was alive and well. The joy of making my first sale on my own was tinged with the regret that I had swindled an old lady out of cash that could have gone into better things.

Later, in the cab home in the glory of the midday sun, I said this to Imsen. She smiled at me. I had thought that she would laugh and tell me how naive I was to feel this way, but she did not. She just smiled said, 'See, that's why I like you, Kris, nothing can change you.' And then, as she rested her head on my shoulder and went off to sleep, she muttered: 'And that's why I love you.'

I reached home with my eyes wide open, wondering if my ears had deceived me or if I was slowly losing it. I chose to believe the latter, took a cold shower and went straight to bed.

The next day, while heading to work, I chose to take the air-conditioned bus instead of the office cab. I wanted time to think and be on my own, even if only for an hour or so. I went over the whole thing in my head. Why would Imsen say that? Did she really say that? Did she mean it? Then I decided that I was acting like a little boy being chased by a lovelorn teen. I was blowing it all out of proportion and overthinking things. Imsen had been sleepy, she probably didn't even remember saying anything.

At work, Imsen acted pretty normal and I breathed a

sigh of relief. It was the last day of the month, which also meant that it was the last day to make data for that month. I was not meeting my sales target, but neither was I sitting on zero. And everything else was in place. As always, I sat next to Imsen and the night flew by in a haze of customers, technical issues and complaints. I realized vaguely that I had not had a conversation with Stan, Dibya or anyone outside of my team in quite a while. Suddenly, there was a lull in call flow and most of the floor sat in queue, waiting to receive calls. After an hour of not getting calls, everyone was getting fidgety. Chiranjib called us all over to his workstation for a team huddle.

'Ok, team, this month has seen a distinct improvement in sales and other parameters. But we can definitely do better. For the last four months, we have been in the bottom five; this month we are in the top five. The management has given us a team outing budget. What shall we do?'

A team outing is a bizarre affair. The company sponsors everything, within a certain budget. While some teams choose to use the opportunity to take a holiday to a beach nearby, some choose to blow it all on food and partying. The bizarre part is that the people you least expect to want to party and drink are the ones who seem to do so more than everyone else. The team decided to party at a disco and everyone, said Chiranjib, had to attend. I was not relishing spending a weekly off-day with office people, but I figured—what the heck—it would be just for a few hours. Besides, Imsen would be there.

When the day came, I wore my faded jeans, a black T-shirt, donned my leather Converses and picked Imsen up. She was dressed simply but looked very hot. Tight black jeans, a white tank top and a short leather jacket made her look awesome. It was too hot for the jacket, so I ended up carrying it. By the time we reached Poison, the disco, the party was in full swing. I recognized my team members, even though I had not bothered to remember their names. The alcohol was free and thus flowing into everyone like water. In order to fully enjoy the drunken celebration of corporate excellence—which was what that the team outing was supposed to be—I'd had Cousin Ty roll me a joint. I thus reached the venue baked right out of my skull.

Imsen had a couple of drinks while making polite conversation with team members. This meant screaming niceties above the din and noise of the disco, which, besides our august group, had its own regulars. After getting thoroughly buzzed, we danced like there was no tomorrow. Imsen and I made a good dancing couple, I thought. Other people danced too, but mostly they glugged down large quantities of alcohol.

The concept of free alcohol seemed to have really motivated everyone into attempting to drink themselves silly. Piyush looked confused about what to do with himself and kept hugging a sozzled Chiranjib. Various others were 'dancing' in Bollywood-hero styles. I noticed all this for about three minutes before Imsen started gyrating against me on the dance floor. The rest of the night went by in a series of dances and vodka shots.

I woke up the next day with a giant hangover and Imsen in my bed. I looked at her sleeping and, for an instant, I thought that it might not be a bad idea to have her over more often. I quickly dispelled this thought when I spied her mobile phone buzzing. According to the screen, her fiancé was calling.

As I walked out of my room to drink some coffee, Ty gave me approving looks and offered me a cigarette I smoked one and read the newspaper, trying to forget the thought that seemed to have taken up permanent residence in my head.

10

THE LONG SHIFT

My designation for the first few months on the production floor was that of a level three technician. Imsen's success with sales was something that remained beyond me. And her talks with her fiancé on the phone still continued. She and I were pretty much going out. Though I pretended it was still a friends-with-benefits situation, I was by now falling hard for her. Also, we had completed about seven months at Big Blue, and her year of living in the big city was drawing to a close.

I chose to forget these things and instead focused on my job and my targets. I often came close to meeting my sales targets but never quite made it. My technical skills and my customer surveys kept saving me from being put into a special focus team. My customer surveys were the best on the floor and I had a spotless record. The quality analysts and the voice coaches on the floor all agreed that I was the best communicator that they had ever audited. My calls were so good, in fact, that they were now being used in training as a sort of guide on what to do.

Chiranjib was very proud of this; so was Piyush. I had become quite famous on the floor because of this. New batches came in and Surya would point me out as the agent whose calls they had heard in training. I was getting my own little spot in the limelight. I had not enjoyed this kind of admiration since my schooldays and I had not realized how much I missed it. Imsen too noticed this; whenever a girl tried to chat me up, she would quickly assert her presence. I only wondered what it all meant and whether she truly meant the words she had said just that once in the cab.

Work remained much the same as usual; the only difference was that I was much faster in resolving issues and found it easier to talk to my faceless American customers. We were facing a manpower shortage on the floor after several people quit in a wave of attrition and we had to do mandatory overtime. This was fine by us because we got paid an extra Rs 1,000 for each day, besides our normal salary. The only problem with working an extra shift was that there was only so much you could put your body through. But I did my overtime and took home my extra cash with no complaints.

Whenever there was an opportunity to make a bonus, I took it. I had already done two OTs—two days of overtime— in the first two weeks of the month. Then, thanks to some political hoohaa in the city, there was a twenty-four hour bandh called by the powers that be. We were told that those who came in to work would have to stay and do an extra shift with double the regular overtime bonus. We were told that there would be food and places to sleep assigned to us. Some people, like me, decided to pull the extra shift. Imsen decided to stay home. Since women were given some preferential treatment, no one objected to this.

When the day actually came, those who stayed back at work took their tired selves to the rooms assigned for sleeping in. The mattresses were smelly and the pillows were no better. The sheets were clean but the odour made it difficult to sleep. Stan started complaining and threatened to go home. Some more people joined in and soon it resembled a labour union strike. When the managers got word that the next shift agents might leave because of the smelly mattresses, they came to placate us with room freshener sprays. Some fat manager we rarely saw even came and slept in the same room just to prove that things were not so bad.

However, this was only the tip of the iceberg. The food given to us for breakfast and lunch was miserable, cold and stale. Some of the eggs were spoilt. I know these complaints sound petty, but when you work a night shift and make the sacrifice of staying back at work just so business requirements can be met, these little things really piss you off. Many people who knew the system better than us newbies did not stay back. Dibya and some other call centre vets did not even show up—they all called in sick.

That day we really did not feel that we worked for an

MNC. Stan joked that we were but slaves building the pharaoh's pyramid. The managers too disappeared in their luxury cars after their little show of solidarity. Only our team leaders and SMEs suffered alongside. At least, Chiranjib and Piyush did; the others were nowhere to be found.

We hunkered down and fought like soldiers at the frontline, stopping only for ten-minute breaks.

When those gruelling forty-eight hours were over, we swore that we would never again take on a shift like that.

The next day, it was business as usual. No one spoke about how bad the conditions had been—the stench in the break room, the rotten food, the insane workload. We only talked about contraceptives: the janitors had cleaned out the clogged toilets to find used condoms jamming up the works. Apparently, a lot of guys on the other teams had made good use of the lumpy 'break time' couches the management had so kindly provided for us.

I was pissed off about people fucking around like that. Then I shrugged. Why grudge people an office lay?

The only good thing that came out of that shift was the extra money we made and a vague recognition among the managers that we were truly committed to the job. Either that or they thought that we were desperate enough to do anything.

Calling continued and work went on with no hope of respite in sight. I knew that sooner or later I had to take a vacation, but whenever I spoke about it to Chiranjib he always asked me to hold out just for that month. Thankfully, we were moved to the seven-thirty shift—which meant that we were be home by five in the morning. It was a great deal better than reaching office in the middle of the night to work the graveyard shift. The flow of work tended to be better during the earlier shifts as well. In an early shift, the calls started as soon as you logged in and slowed down as the shift progressed; but in a later shift the calls started as a trickle and then became a flood as the shift grew older and the agents tired.

After taking calls for almost six months, I started noticing that customers were now calling in saying that they had received alerts from our software or emails from us telling them that their security was missing a key component. On remote-checking their computers, I would often come up with nothing. To mask the fact that the mails were some sort of marketing ploy, I made a big show of cleaning up and optimizing their computer. I checked if the others had received such calls; most people had.

I asked Dibya what he was doing with such calls and he grinned at me. 'Selling to them, man. It's a golden opportunity! They call in scared, I use Badware Bytes and scare them some more. And then I sell them McCurseSpree for three years.'

It was ingenious if you thought about it. We had customers' information and their trust. By mailing them and alerting them of 'potential' security threats, we were doing our job; by exposing their 'viruses', existent or non-existent, we were getting easy sales.

'What if they already have McCurseSpree?' I asked Dibya. 'Then what do you sell?'

'Heh, then it's either the warranty plan for three years, using the manual virus clean-ups as a selling point, or the hardware warranty by telling them that their computer's hardware is being corrupted by the virus.'

Dibya was an evil genius, and his sales figures stood testament to it. He was making close to Rs 50,000 every time the sales incentives were being doled out. In fact, he was among the highest earners on the floor. As one agent put it: 'The firangs stole from us for 200 years with violence and war. We will get it all back using technology and our mouths.'

We were actually looting our American customers, selling them things they did not need. But it was either us or the competition, and we were way better than our competitors. Take TechBuddha, for example. They claimed universal software knowledge and were our closest competitors in the technical support market. However, their agents knew nothing about how to fix someone's computer and focused only on sales. We sold too, but we did our jobs when it came to fixing stuff. We were, in a sense, 'ethical' conmen.

Using Dibya's tips, I started selling more. After adding my own creative twists with some customers, I started to sell regularly.

'Your computer has a lot of viruses. Viruses are a backdoor

for hackers who use them to steal your information, especially your credit card information. They sell your credit card information to others. I will clean your computer up for you, but you need to buy stronger protection for your computer today. Let me see if I have something that will do the job for you.'

In my heart, I knew that what I was doing was wrong. But just like a white lie is somewhere between a lie and the truth, sales is somewhere in between desperation and sheer con artistry. It was never greed that pushed us to sell; it was our team leaders and our SMEs, whose own stacks depended on the overall team performance. This, in turn, was demanded by their superiors—higher management.

Higher management. The nameless, faceless entities who came to the office in luxury cars, followed by yesmen. They were rumoured to take home bonuses that ran in crores. There was a clear path to reaching their position, and each step involved getting better at different skills. However, the first promotion was the most difficult to get because the entire floor was competing. When we were told that a new level of technician would be recruited from the floor itself, everyone suddenly threw their game into high gear.

The criterion for qualifying for the level four super-tech job was simple: we had to meet floor data, which meant that we had to sell like never before. In a month's time, there would be written exams for those who qualified, then an interview round for those who passed the exams. This was, as Dibya put it, 'a golden-diamond-platinum opportunity'. Stan more accurately declared: 'The rat race has begun.' Only Imsen was unsure and not really competing. She was nearing the end of her year in the big city and a promotion was meaningless for her.

I did not know what to do. It was very clear to me now that I had serious feelings for her.

After four weeks of selling and pushing ourselves to the limit, we had a shortlist of 100, out of the 400 people who took calls. We had a technical test to sit for, after which we would go through an IJP. Unlike other promotions, where not just skill but initiative was also a criterion, here we did not have to do anything more than fulfilling our already existing job criteria. And, in return, we were to become the technicians' technician. We would not sell any more and, supported by a team of trainers, we would provide solutions to technical issues which nobody else would touch with a ten-foot pole. To qualify, though, we would not only have to pass the exam and the interviews but also a take refresher training course, where we would be trained on third-party software and other advanced issues. It sounded like quite a task, but most of us were tired of sales. We were willing to take the extra burden of constant learning to evade the trap of selling.

Piyush came over to my workstation while I was on a call and gestured to me to put my call on mute. 'You have made the shortlist, and so have you Imsen,' he said.

I was not surprised—Imsen met her targets regularly, even though she wasn't really trying.

The 100 hopefuls were seated at different computers preloaded with a set of online tests. I did alright on mine. I'm no Bill Gates, but I was hopeful of passing. Imsen flashed me the victory sign and Stan called me to take a smoke break with him.

Instead of heading outside to the smoking area, Stan led me to the stairwell. A lot of moaning and groaning could be heard there. Stan grinned. 'That's just the usual these days. Couples getting it on. But we're heading for something else.' Down below, a group was waiting for Stan, who grinned and produced a small pouch. Stan had apparently formed a small bunch of stoners who took their breaks together and got high. I recognized Wribhu in the dark and a few others from the floor; however, I had not expected to see my team leader there.

'So how was the exam, Kris?' Chiranjib asked in between pulls of a fat joint that someone had rolled.

'It went well. I hope I get called for the interview.'

'No worries, Kris. I've already spoken to the assessors. It seems they are fans of yours and have heard your calls which are used in training. It's a sure thing.'

This was a bigger surprise than the fact that I had just discovered that my team leader was a stoner. I had not imagined that I was a sure shot for the new level four technical team. I felt good for the first time since I had joined Big Blue—I finally felt like I was going somewhere. It's not something that most people who work at call centres will readily give voice to, but the truth is that we feel like losers most of the time.

We work six days a week at night shifts for a pitiful salary, not knowing when we will get our weekly off-day, and we get yelled at for every stupid thing. And taking calls is a monotonous and stressful thing—most people can only take calls for a maximum of three years before they quit or, hopefully, move into a higher position. I was hoping to get into the level four team not only because sales would no longer be a criterion but also because of the higher pay grade. This would have been a long shot otherwise because I had just the bare minimum experience required to sit for an IJP. After what Chiranjib had said, I was feeling very positive.

I went in for my interview with a lot of expectations. I was even wearing formals for the occasion. I had an off that day, so I had come to the office just for my interview. While I waited outside the training room that would double as the interview venue, Imsen texted me: 'Looking very handsome in formals. Good luck with your interview.' I smiled to myself as I waited my turn, trying to remember all the technical questions that might be asked or the process-related ones that might crop up.

There were just three people on the interview panel: Natarajan, the fat manager who had slept on the smelly mattresses; Anju Reddy, who had conducted my voice and accent interview; and Surya, my former technical trainer. All I got asked was: 'So, what's the northeast like this time of year?'

My interview might have been a farce, but I got a place on the level four team—that's all that mattered to me. Imsen, Dibya, Wribhu and Stan congratulated me and started asking for a treat, which meant drinking. Dibya had also cleared his interview and would be in the same team as me. There were just ten of us in the first level four team. We were to be the pilot team, which would be used as a test to see how well customers would take to having more advanced technicians serving them.

After a five-day training session by Surya, comprising presentations on networking, virus removal, registry tricks and tips and some more third-party software gyaan, we were put into operation. Since we had a small team, initially we would only do an opening five-thirty shift. Since we were a product and our services had to be bought in order for us to get a call, we had plenty of time to kick back our heels. Other teams logged in and took calls while we provided support when we were not on call. For a brief while, we were the stars on the floor. We reported directly to Natarajan and Surya provided us technical support, so no problem was too great for us.

We were making more money, taking fewer calls, had more free time and got more respect. But, like all good things, this too came to an end. We were assigned a new team leader and new targets to meet. The targets were not a problem, but our new team leader was. By now, the stairwell was my new home, complete with background sex sounds and the litter of condoms of the dotted and/ or ribbed variety—little did I know that my happy stoner days were about to be rudely interrupted.

11

THE TEAM LEADER FROM HELL

The concept of the level four technician was that we were the best of the best. When a customer had an issue that could not be solved by a regular technician, after confirmation from his SME or team leader the agent could sell the level four option. The level four option cost $79 and was valid for a one-month period. If the problem recurred within one month, we would work on it as many times as needed, within that one-month span. Level four technicians had a certain number of cases that they had to solve in a month. This was our resolution rate. The other targets, like average handling time, etc., remained the same.

The one target that had become important now that we were pure technicians was the customer satisfaction survey. Our bonuses and incentives were judged by all the factors I mentioned, but the survey was king. To get a positive survey, we had to be outstanding on the call, not just in terms of technical knowhow but also in terms of customer service. We had to ensure that the customer was satisfied, which was not easy. They came to us after exhausting all possible options, and they were tired, angry and frustrated, not to mention short of $79.

Our task was to make them happy and get their problem solved. If the problem was not solved, not only would we get a 'Dissat' but also earn a refund. If more than five refunds came against a particular agent, his stack incentives for the month were gone; but if the refund was attributed or judged to be caused by the agents, then it was straight to the firing squad.

We managed to find a fool-proof way of preventing the survey from being sent, if so needed. The survey was only generated if we started a remote session or started working on the computer. When we disconnected the session, the survey was sent; but if we shut down the customer's computer and then ended the session, the survey was blocked. This was traceable if the quality analysts on the floor watched the screenshots and the recordings. However, if a customer was disgruntled, then the survey block was a must-do. The risk was that if the quality analysts caught you, they could get you fired if they wanted to.

Everything was running fine till the day we started experiencing a massive surge in call volumes. Suddenly, every agent worth his headset was selling level four support and we were drowning in calls. Some of the technical issues we were getting were easily solvable. For instance, if someone's computer kept freezing, whatever the reason, it could easily be solved by an operating system reinstallation.

But the lower level agents were passing on such cases to us; they were feigning their inability to solve such cases to meet increased sales targets and their supervisors were giving the go-ahead to save their own incentives. We level four agents were taking the brunt of the customers' anger when they saw how easily solvable their problems were and we were reaping a harvest of refunds on most days.

By the end of the month, our team data was in the red, something which had not happened in the first month of operations. Management thus decided that they would not stem the flow of dollars that were coming as result of these sales; but they had to stem the flow of refunds. So they also decided to track our surveys, as they were the best indicators of our performance on the call. In order to make us perform better, they appointed Manjeet Kaur as our team leader.

Manjeet Kaur had already gathered a reputation as a total psycho. Uncle Biswajeet and Stan, who had suffered in his team, told us to watch out. Not only would he make us extend our shifts but also call us in on our off-days for extra training. Being singled out for his attention was a terrible fate. As if this were not enough, he was also very abusive. Try listening nine hours of someone reciting 'Teri maa behn ek kardoonga', and you will an idea of how he was. Even Surya, who was acting as our SME, was wary of him.

However, when Manjeet took our first team huddle, he seemed like a different person altogether. We were very taken aback and suspected that something was certainly up.

'Now, people, let's work together and get those Csats—the customer satisfaction surveys—up. The refunds I can take care of, but in return I want those Csats to be positive.'

This we interpreted as: 'The refunds do not matter to me because they affect your stack, not mine; but get those Csats because they affect my stack.' The game here was pretty simple: as long as we kept our Csats in the green, he would manipulate the refunds and get them attributed to those who were selling.

For the first month, everything went well. Not only were the refunds few and far between but the Csats were piling in. All this was not happening without effort, mind you. We were totally buttering up the customers. We used all the conversational skills we had to make the customer feel like we were doing our best. We made them part of our lives, even if only for a brief while. Some of them even forgot their problems, but I guess sweet-talking can do that.

In the meantime, my personal life was going to hell all over again. Imsen's fiancé had decided to take a holiday from work and visit her for a week.

I tried to tell myself that it was just a week and that we had nothing special between us. But when she took that week off from work to spend time with her fiancé, I almost went crazy. I felt like I was losing her, like I had lost my chance at happiness. I knew in my heart that I loved her, that she was the one. The only problem was that her mobile was switched off, so I could not call her. I decided to go to her apartment and talk to her. I was willing to take a chance and tell her how I felt.

After a shift of calls and Csats sweet-talk for the customers, I made my way to her flat. I rang the bell, but no one answered. I tried again and again, but still no one answered. I tried calling her mobile; it was still switched off. I thought of leaving her a note, but decided against it.

I was at my wits' end. And it certainly showed at work.

Usually, I got maybe two or three Dissats in a month; now I was getting them every week. My positive surveys were also falling. Manjeet took me to a corner and tried to motivate me in his own inimitable way.

'Listen, you asshole. I don't care what the hell is wrong with you. You are killing the team's data, and your own. If you don't get your act together, I will fuck your happiness! You get me, you bastard?' Then he added some more abuse for good effect.

I felt like kicking Manjeet's ass right there on the production floor, but he was right. I was screwing my data and I had to fix it. Some things might be beyond me, but some things I still had control over. This did not mean that I was not angry with Manjeet. He had finally started showing his true colours.

In the time that Imsen was away from me, I realized that I did not give a crap about the call centre. The incentives and the money were worthless. The promotions were also empty. After all, even a manager had to come in to work at night like a watchman. My call centre felt like Sodom and

Gomorrah rolled into one without Imsen. With everyone willing to do just about anything to get ahead, the only reason everything had been tolerable so far was that she was there with me.

With Imsen gone, I could see people for what they really were. The team leaders for the money-hungry fools they were, and the agents who were conmen pretending to be technicians. However, to keep Manjeet off my back, I pushed myself. Call it negative motivation, but it worked.

Within a week, I had my data under control again, with Csats balancing Dissats to keep my data green. I had still not heard from Imsen. I had been to her apartment a couple of times again to find that no one was there. I asked her neighbours, but they had no idea where she could be. I finally asked Chiranjib if he had heard from Imsen.

'She called me saying that she needs to extend her leave as she has to go for a wedding in Siliguri, but why do you want to know?' said Chiranjib.

I walked off without replying. It seemed possible enough that Imsen might be at a relative's wedding, but inside my head alarm bells were ringing. 'It's her wedding. She's gone. You had your chance and you blew it.'

I pinged Stan on the office messenger. 'Dude, I'm so stressed.'

'I got a way to cure that, haha. Meet me at the stairwell.'

So I took a break, knowing full well what Stan was suggesting. By now, he had a reputation on the production floor as the resident druggie—this was a slight exaggeration.

All he ever did was get stoned—no hard drugs of any kind. And since a couple of managers and team leaders smoked with him, he was fully protected.

At the stairwell, Stan produced a joint and lit it. 'Best stuff in Kolkata, bro. From Bondel Gate.'

I smirked. I had smoked hash with Ty—and nothing could be better than that. Within twenty minutes, though, the smirk was wiped off my face. I was feeling like I was moving in slow motion and had difficulty walking. Everything slowed down to a crawl.

Stan smiled. 'Stress relief much, bro?'

I was so stoned I could not give a shit about anything any more. Manjeet could drown in a sea of Dissats, for all I cared. They could fire me, and I would not even blink an eyelid. Nothing mattered.

Stan grabbed me by my hand before I could leave. 'Some Clearin for your eyes, bro. Them eyes are red as hell.'

Stan was a smart stoner. The weed generally made your eyes red and puffy. Clearin was an eye drop that solved that problem. The rest depended on how much you could control your high.

When Stan and I got back to the production floor, Manjeet was screaming at the whole team. I wondered what was wrong.

'Conference room! Team huddle now, you fuckers!' he yelled.

This was the last thing I wanted to do when stoned, but I followed Dibya anyway, knowing full well that Manjeet was about to unload all his venom on us. Usually, he ranted at someone right on the floor; if he was calling you to a private room, you could expect a tongue-lashing the likes of which you had probably not received since you were a kid. It was not that other team leaders did not yell at their teams; but everyone had a certain limit—Manjeet had none.

Everyone trooped into the conference room, one after the other, like lambs to the slaughter. I was so stoned I could not care what he did or wanted from us. Once the door closed, he launched into his finest performance thus far.

'You assholes, motherfuckers, bastards! All I ask is for you to keep your Csats up, yet you keep fucking up. What's missing, huh? Do I not save your useless asses when you get multiple refunds? You, Kris! Have I not saved you from being fired?'

'Um, yeah. You have, Manjeet,' I mumbled.

'In return, all I have asked for is steady Csats, which you are giving me. But what the fuck is wrong with the rest of you? Answer me!' screamed Manjeet as my eardrums gently melted and my buzz faded in and out.

'Well, some of the Dissats came because the customers were not happy with the solutions,' said Dibya.

'Oh, YEAH. Well, whose job is it to make sure the customer is happy, huh? Mine or yours?' snapped Manjeet.

Dibya had just opened his mouth to speak when, suddenly, Manjeet strode over to him, grabbed his collar and slapped him.

We were stunned. Abuses were okay up to a point, but this was physical assault.

Dibya pushed Manjeet away and walked out. We saw him heading straight to a manager's cabin, no doubt to register a complaint.

Big Blue had very strict rules about abuse. The rules were bent when it came to verbal abuse, but laying your hand on someone was a big no-no.

Surya poked his head in through the door and asked, 'What's happening?'

'Nothing,' growled Manjeet. Then he went out and followed Dibya into the manager's room.

While I briefed Surya about what had just happened the rest of the team looked on in silence.

Surya sent us back to the floor to take calls and finish our shift. We all wondered what would happen now, but Manjeet and Dibya did not come out till the shift was over. Finally, down at the transport bay, while I waited for my cab, a red-faced and visibly angry Dibya came over to me.

'We have to fix him,' he said.

'How do we do that?'

'Let me handle that. Are you with me?

'Sure,' I said, wondering what Dibya had up his sleeve.

I was still a bit high and, as the cab headed home, I realized that there were two things on my mind. Imsen and her wedding trip were giving me the jitters; at the same time, I really wanted Manjeet out of my hair so that I could get back to work without being abused constantly.

In the meantime, however, there were the team parties to attend. This meant litres of alcohol at Oly Pub, many sticks of weed or hash, and subsequently ending up in bed with people you only knew professionally. I never did that, but plenty of people were quite happy to do it. This was the normal scene.

The real madness happened at the client parties, where the managers would invite some pretty candidates to 'entertain' the clients. The clients brought new processes and the girls were usually keen to be 'useful'. It was a win-win for everyone. The clients got laid, the company got more business and the girls got promoted.

12

HOW TO ELIMINATE A TEAM LEADER

The agents were often told that we were the real assets of a call centre. We took calls and made sales while everyone else was there to give us support and make sure things ran smoothly. Without us, the whole machinery would fall apart. Of course, this did not mean that we were untouchable, but the management would think twice before firing us. This was the concept that Dibya laid out in front of me. Our Csat percentage was fixed at 60 per cent, which meant that we had the space to get Dissats without fear of reprisal. Our venerable team leader's Csat percentage was 70 per cent, which meant that his team had the space to get only 30 per cent Dissats.

A 70 per cent target for Csats was doable because if one member started doing badly someone else could cover for him or her. Also the option to shut down the customer's computer to prevent the survey from being sent out was freely exercised by the team members when they felt a Dissat was on its way. These factors were saving Manjeet's bacon. But, if we chose to, we could send his data down the drain.

And that was exactly what we were going to do. For two weeks, we screwed his data and started getting six Csats and four Dissats every week. Manjeet noticed this and started doing heat checks. A heat check was when a supervisor took over a call and verified whether a survey would come back as a positive or a negative. This was a way of raising a flag and anticipating a Dissat; but Manjeet started forcing us to shut down computers to prevent surveys from going out.

We thought that our whole idea might just sink. The concept on the whole was brilliant—we were utilizing the system to eliminate someone we did not see fit to lead us. However, Manjeet started seeing the trends in the data very early and began pushing us to prevent the surveys. We were facing a long-term haul with Manjeet as our team leader and the thought made us groan in anguish.

When Imsen returned to the office after two weeks of silence, she pinged me on the office messenger, saying, 'We need to talk.' I tried to find out what had happened, but Manjeet kept looming over my shoulder. I decided to wait till later, though my mind was coming up with a million possibilities.

'Maybe she got married in Siliguri. That's why she came back so late,' I thought to myself while my customer kept on asking me what was wrong with his computer. I told the customer that I would continue working on his computer through the remote session and offered to disconnect the call. We did this if we did not feel like talking to the customer or buttering them for a Csat. We called them once the work was done to close the case. Usually we just ran scans to pass the time and make the customer think we were working.

I ran a long scan on the customer computer and pinged Imsen, asking her to take a break. Dibya looked at me as if to say 'What the fuck are you doing?' No one left a computer and went off during a remote session. We were allowed to kill time but not leave the workstation. I asked Dibya to watch my system for a few minutes while I went out to meet Imsen.

As I walked the shiny corridors to the cafe outside where she waited for me, I thought about what I wanted to say to her. I had been over this many a time in my head, the moment of my confession of my love for her. I saw her sitting at a table. The cup of coffee in front of her was untouched. She looked almost exactly like the day I had first met her: beautiful, radiant and calm. But this time there was something more. She glowed as if with an inner light.

'Long time no see, Imsen,' I said, trying to act as if I did not give a shit. Inside, I wanted to scream at her tell her how much I missed her, ask her where she had been, why her phone was switched off. Most of all, I wanted to tell her that I loved her. Instead of all that, I sat in front of her, pretending to be cool and ordering myself a cold coffee. I was doing my best to appear unflappable.

'I'm sorry I did not call you,' Imsen said. 'My mobile got stolen and I had to attend my cousin's wedding in Siliguri.'

That solved two mysteries. But where did her fiancé fit into this?

'I missed you,' I said, trying not to sound like a lovelorn schoolboy.

Imsen smiled fleetingly.

The questions I wanted to ask were simple. Would she stay on in Kolkata even though her year was over? Would she marry her fiancé? Did she love me or was it just an arrangement that was convenient for both of us?

It was now or never. I was about to ask, when she spoke.

'Kris, I am pregnant?'

'What?' I exclaimed.

'It's yours,' she said.

My mind drew up a picture of me with a baby swaddled in clothes, feeding that baby, becoming a husband and a father in one fell stroke. My brain went into atomic meltdown mode.

'But how can you be sure? After all, your fiancé...' No sooner were the words out of my mouth than I regretted them instantly.

'I haven't been with anyone else, you fool!' she hissed.

I was seeing Imsen angry for the first time, and truth be told she scared me just a little. Then she got up in a huff and walked away. I followed her, asking her to stop, but she walked right out of the café, out of the office compound and into a taxi.

I was wondering whether I should follow or not when Manjeet clamped a hand on my shoulder.

'Kris, you have exceeded your break for the hundredth time this week. What's the matter?'

I wanted to say, 'Oh, nothing much. My girlfriend whom I love but who is engaged to someone else is pregnant with my baby. I am about to become a father and I am shitting myself. That's all.' Instead, I walked wordlessly back to the floor to take calls.

Once my shift was over, I went straight to Imsen's flat. But the door was locked and her phone was still unreachable. I cursed myself for being such a dimwit.

What was I to do? Imsen was preggers, I had a job but one that could hardly support a family, why did she not have an abortion, would I have to marry her now? And then I wondered whether she wanted me to marry her or not. In order to answer my questions, I had to find her first.

During the next shift, I looked around to see if she had come to work. She wasn't there. I asked Dibya whether he knew how to get into employee records. He told me that someone in human resources might be able to help. I knew no one in HR, so I did the next best thing. I walked into the trainer's room and sought out Anju Reddy.

'Hi, I need some help.' I said.

'With what, Kris?' she said, giving me an appraising look.

'I need someone's number. She is not using her usual number. I know that she must have given her home number when she submitted her documents. Can you help me?' I pleaded, making my best puppy-dog face.

She grimaced at me. 'Look, that sort of information is classified. I can't look into Imsen's records just like that. Why don't you try asking her team leader? He might have some information.'

'Um. How do you know it's her?'

'I'm not blind, you know. And everyone on the floor can tell something's up between the two of you.' She smiled. 'Okay, since I like you, tell you what, give me a day and I will have the number.'

I could have kissed her in gratitude. I went back to calls with a smile on my face.

The whole team was sitting silently in our bay. 'No calls?' I asked.

'No, we are off calls for the moment. Manjeet has been called in by the managers,' Dibya responded.

Though I wanted to know what was happening, I was more anxious about getting Imsen's contact details. I hoped and prayed that Anju Reddy would pull through for me.

Moments later, Manjeet emerged from the manager's cabin. His face was red with rage. He strode straight over to where we were seated and started screaming at the top of his lungs. 'You bastards! You fuckfaces! You backstabbing assholes! You think you have gotten the better of me, have you? Just wait till I get you in my team again. I will personally hound the lot of you into resigning. I promise you this, you behnchods!'

Dibya looked straight at him and said, 'Fuck off.'

This enraged Manjeet even further and he lunged. However, the team members managed to grab him before he could get to Dibya. A huge ruckus erupted on the floor and security was called in. Manjeet was escorted off the floor.

Dibya calmly walked over to everyone and said, 'Thanks, guys. That piece of shit will never bother us again.'

The management had taken Manjeet off the team following a drop in his data and several complaints against him. The complaints were nothing new; however, since he was no longer an asset, he was also expendable. Dibya had managed to pull it off.

In the process, though, we had become notorious on the floor. Everyone now looked at us as if we were capable of anything. We may have gotten one team leader off our backs, but now every team leader looked at us as if we were the enemy.

But I could be least bothered about all this. All I wanted to do was to go to Anju and get the information I wanted. During the next shift at work, I took a break and walked over to her room. Anju handed me a sheet of paper and said, 'You owe me one.'

I did not know how she intended to get any favours out of me, but I took the sheet. I scanned through it. It had Imsen's home address and home number.

Since it was five in the morning, I was willing to wager that no one would pick up the phone. I decided to wait till I got home to try and call her family to find out where she was.

Waiting is the worst part of any punishment that one may have to endure. While I waited and waited and waited, an endless loop of thoughts played in my head. I was regretting my words greatly. How could I have been stupid enough to even suggest that the baby might not be mine? I hoped she hadn't lost her temper and done anything rash. I had no past experience to compare her temper with—after all, she had never been angry with me before. One thought stood out clearly: I wanted to be with her. I had feelings for her—getting married to her would not be such a bad thing.

I reached home. Cousin Ty was sitting on the sofa and watching TV. I had not expected him to be home.

'Hey, bro, what's up?' he said. 'You got a smoke?'

I pulled out my pack of smokes and sat down beside him. He was watching some old Chinese kung fu flick, where the heroes were flying around and the heroines were all kick-ass. He was also stoned out of his wits.

'You're home early?'

'Yup.' Ty's face was grim.

'What's wrong?' I asked.

'I got fired, Kris.'

Ty used to smoke up on a regular basis in office. There was a whole gang of them at work. They took bike trips together to a bunker somewhere in North Kolkata to buy hash, often ending up in a place called Bhootnath to buy chillums or smoke bongs. Today, all of a sudden, the lockers of the entire office had been raided. And since Ty kept all his junk in his locker, he had been summarily fired.

The reason for the raid turned out to be pretty terrible. One of the office junkies had crashed his bike during a drug-fuelled drag race. Seated behind was an office girl who had accompanied them for a thrill. The girl had lost her life, a police case had ensued and the office management had suddenly become aware that there were stoners and junkies in their midst. And Ty had become the unfortunate scapegoat. I felt sorry for him.

'Why do you have such a long face, bro?' he asked me.

'Oh, nothing much.' I lied and walked off to my room to try and reach Imsen at home. The dial tone kept coming back as busy, so I decided to go over to her flat yet again and see if she was there.

I stood outside the flat, groggy and sleepy but hopeful that she might be in. No such luck. The flat was locked.

I tried calling her home number again. After many tries, finally someone picked up.

'Hello?' A female voice answered.

'Hello,' I said. 'My name is Kris. Is Imsen home?' I spoke slowly, just in case the lady on the other end did not understand English.

'You don't have to talk to me like I'm deaf or an idiot,' she snapped. 'I am Imsen's mother. What do you want?'

'Well, her phone's switched off and she has not come to the office in a couple of days. So I was worried and...'

'Okay, okay. No need to worry. Imsen is at her aunt's place in Howrah. Wait, I'll give you her number. You call her, okay? Imsen's mother said.

I breathed a sigh of relief, like a constipated man taking a dump after a week.

I could now find Imsen, speak to her, make her understand, beg her for forgiveness, confess my love for her in no uncertain terms.

I took down the number gratefully, thanking her mother profusely for giving a stranger her daughter's number. I called the number immediately, but a man's voice answered.

'Hi, I'm looking for Imsen,' I said.

'And who are you?' asked the man.

'My name is Kris. It is very important that I talk to her,' I replied.

I could hear talking in the background after that. I could make out Imsen's voice—she sounded angry and defiant. I hoped I was not talking to her fiancé.

'Well, she says that she does not want to talk to you,' the man finally said to me.

'Please do me a favour? Give me your address, and I will come there. If she still does not want to talk to me, then I will not bother you again.'

The man cut the call. I sat down weary and sad. I had lost her. Because of my own stupidity. I cursed my fate over and over again.

My mobile buzzed a minute later. I had received a

message that said: 'Sorry, I had to cut the call. I am Imsen's cousin.' The address followed in the next text.

I hurried into a taxi and rushed towards the address on my phone screen. My heart was in my mouth. I hoped that I could persuade her to forgive me. I hoped I could make things right.

As the taxi sped along the roads of Kolkata, I thought of how the city had changed in the years that I had been there. The familiar hangouts at New Market no longer bustled as they used to, malls were springing up everywhere I looked. Kolkata was no longer as sleepy as before. However, the more things changed the more they remained the same. The people were still the same. Only I had changed.

I knew now that I was no longer the same naive boy who had come to the city to have a good time. I worked hard to make my money. I worked nights, chased targets and lived up to my commitments.

If there was one thing that I had learnt in all this time, it was that I had to find a line of work that could sustain me and my future family. My small salary and dubious job could not satisfy me any longer. I had a dream now: a small one, a goal I wanted to achieve. I wanted Imsen in the worst possible way—not just to love but to have for life and beyond.

The taxi ground to a halt next to a housing complex. It was dark by now and the paths were lit by the streetlights. I paid the driver, found the right door and rang the bell.

Nobody answered.

I rang again and again, hoping that I was not at the wrong flat.

The door finally opened to reveal Imsen, sullen-eyed and angry.

'I am so sorry… Please forgive what I said…' Mustering up my courage, I croaked: 'I love you'.

At that, Imsen punched me and knocked me out.

When I came to, I found a young guy sporting a shiner identical to mine. It was Imsen's cousin.

Imsen looked angry still. 'I'm getting married—and you choose now of all times to show up?'

I had no idea what to say, so I listened as she ranted on and on about how I had left her in the lurch, how she could not do this to her fiancé, how his family honour was on the line, and how she could not trust me.

All I could do was hang my head in shame. 'I know I was wrong to accuse you of anything,' I finally said. 'I should have not said what I said. I've been looking for you. I tried calling you…'

Silence greeted my words.

'I want you. I love you. If you will take me, then I will spend the rest of my life proving it to you.'

Admittedly, it was not the best apology ever. Imsen did not have any tears in her eyes or a smile on her face. She simply stared at me and said, 'Okay, then. If you love me, what do you plan to do about this situation?'

I was stumped. There weren't really many options.

'Let me talk to your parents and explain the situation,' I said.

'And who will explain it to my fiancé?' she yelled.

'Look,' I said. 'I'm trying to make things right. I don't have all the answers, but I want you to be with me.'

I think we must have sat there for a good while, not saying anything. Finally, Imsen sighed.

'Let me pack my bags and let's get out of here. I'll call my parents, but you'll have to talk to them and explain everything.'

And so, just like that, in true *DDLJ* style, we boarded a taxi and eloped, while her cousin stood by sheepishly. I did not even know the poor guy's name, I realized.

Everything seemed to be falling in place. I held Imsen's hand and gripped it tight while the taxi sped along the lanes of Howrah. The lights, the darkness and the empty roads all spoke of a bright new future to me. I looked at her and smiled.

13

KRIS, THE CALL CENTRE WORKER

I still keep in touch with Stan, Dibya and Wribhu. They still work at Big Blue. Dibya is a team leader now and Stan is his SME; they both work stoned as always. Wribhu is a voice and accent trainer and he loves his work. The process we worked for folded after allegations of fraud and 'scareware' by many customers. The software we installed also installed the fake viruses that we used as selling points, and some customers had finally caught on. But Big Blue came up with something else soon enough and was back in business just weeks later.

After Imsen and I decided to get hitched, she put in her papers. We weren't allowed to 'fraternize' with colleagues. Besides, working night shifts is not good for a mother to-be. While we wait for the baby, Imsen is making plans to study further. Or maybe sing. We try not to think too much about the unpleasant encounter when we met her parents—it wasn't that they weren't willing to bless us; her fiancé's whole family had turned up to demand an explanation for the situation. I feel lucky to have escaped unscathed, with only a bruise or two.

I quit Big Blue shortly after the level four technician process went bust. I didn't want to be there without Imsen, my anchor, the woman who gives meaning to my life. But, of course, I had to join another call centre immediately after. With a baby on the way, one has to make a living howsoever one can.

Turns out, life has no big purpose for me to discover; nor do I have any big dreams to fulfil. Only small ones that need to come true, and that suits me just fine. With the coming of new life, I feel perhaps that this is the role I was meant to play. I am, after all, one of the nameless, faceless masses who inhabit this country of ours, who live life at night, hidden away from the eyes of the daylight world. Perhaps the purpose of my life is to make sure that my child has one. Perhaps this is all one can expect out of life—to find love, to live somewhat happily, to hopefully not have to work at a call centre for too long.

Previously published…

CONFESSIONS OF
A PRIVATE TUTOR

VIKRAM MATHUR

A man starts giving maths tuitions to keep his family afloat.
But with the students come their mothers. Voluptuous.
Willing. Moneyed.

My father calculated my bus fare to college and added
a hundred rupees a month as emergency money,
just in case I needed to come home by taxi. If I spent any
of my emergency money, I had to explain why or repay
him. In three months' time, I was in debt and the fights
were getting regular. That's when I decided that I would
give tuitions in mathematics. It's a subject I know. It's also
a subject which has a steady demand. I didn't know at that
point if I could teach it, but I did know that there was a
market. Three years later, I was doing pretty well at it. I
made enough money to bribe and seduce and impress a
girl—I shall call her Sunayana and beg her pardon should
she be reading this—so much that she actually allowed
me to lick her cunt.

April 2013

Coming soon…

CONFESSIONS OF
A PAGE 3 REPORTER

MEGHA MALHOTRA

An ambitious and attractive girl lands herself a job as a Page 3 journalist with a leading daily in New Delhi. The glamour has her friends in thrall, but the vicious politicking is not what journalism school had prepared her for.

We journalists make for an interesting breed, you know? Nowhere else will you find people so happy to get together and bitch their heads off about the profession they chose to be in. Too little pay, punishing hours, overbearing know-it-all colleagues—all of this to bring you ignorant masses education and entertainment! If we are not the unsung soldiers of this world then who is? It's only the perks which keep us Page 3 journalists tied to our jobs. For, who wouldn't kill to attend a Fatboy Slim concert for free, that too VIP/Press seating? Who wouldn't want go in for a chit-chat with the visiting celeb from B-town? And even if you are truly evolved and care little for cheap thrills, you will surely not be indifferent to those fancy wine-tasting dos you get to review. But, to get ahead, you have to 'compromise'…

June 2013